"It's gone!" Gloria gasped, fear spreadin through her like an icy wave.

"What's gone?" Nancy asked. "What's the matter with you, Gloria? You look pale."

Gloria's knees felt wobbly. " I...how could it have..." Her he was having trouble t am I going to do hout

"Gloria," permission,

Just then S their conversation, burs gave Nancy a sly smile. "I think I ight have happened to your necklace," s d.

"What?" Gloria exclaimed.

"Well, I can't prove anything, of course, but I ran into your friend Angie a few minutes ago, and she was putting something into her purse that she didn't want me to see."

SENIORS

Ask your bookseller for any you have missed:

1. TOO MUCH, TOO SOON
2. SMART ENOUGH TO KNOW
3. WINNER ALL THE WAY
4. AFRAID TO LOVE
5. BEFORE IT'S TOO LATE
6. TOO HOT TO HANDLE
7. HANDS OFF, HE'S MINE
8. FORBIDDEN KISSES
9. A TOUCH OF GINGER
10. PRESENTING SUPERHUNK
11. BAD GIRL
12. DON'T SAY GOOD-BYE

SUPER SENIORS™

OLD ENOUGH

Created by Eileen Goudge

BANTAM BOOKS

TORONTO • NEW YORK • LONDON • SYDNEY • AUCKLAND

To Robin

OLD ENOUGH
A BANTAM BOOK 0 553 17636 6

First publication in Great Britain

PRINTING HISTORY
Bantam edition published 1989

Bantam Books are published by Transworld Publishers Ltd., 61–63 Uxbridge Road, Ealing, London W5 5SA, in Australia by Transworld Publishers (Australia) Pty. Ltd., 15–23 Helles Avenue, Moorebank, NSW 2170, and in New Zealand by Transworld Publishers (N.Z.) Ltd., Cnr. Moselle and Waipareira Avenues, Henderson, Auckland.

Printed and bound in Great Britain by Cox & Wyman Ltd., Reading, Berks.

Chapter One

Gloria Larsen held up the dripping, yowling Siamese kitten.

"You poor thing." She grabbed a towel to wrap it in, then turned her attention to the five-year-old twins standing in a puddle of water before the bathroom sink. "Mickey, Mandy . . . what happened?"

Mickey stuck his thumb in his mouth, staring up at her with innocent blue eyes. It was Mandy who explained in her babyish lisp, "We jutht gave kitty a bath!"

Gloria was dismayed. This mischievous pair was going to make her late for the meeting at which the biggest event of the entire summer was being mapped out. Tomorrow was the first day of Senior Orientation Weekend, and she'd volunteered to help.

A lot of the kids coming up from Glenwood were her friends, and she was dying to see them again after a whole summer away from home.

Gloria finished rubbing the kitten dry and gently placed it on the floor. As it skittered off, its fur sticking up in damp tufts, Mickey and Mandy broke into peals of delighted laughter.

Gloria laughed, too. The twins were awfully cute, even when they were being devilish.

"Just behave yourselves until I get back," she warned them, "or you'll get *me* in hot water with Mrs. Daniels." The old housekeeper had been reluctant to take over Gloria's job for a few hours. She didn't need the twins misbehaving as well.

"We'll be good," Mandy promised, darting a playful glance at Mickey. She skipped out of the room, her twin brother, his thumb firmly planted in his mouth, trailing behind.

Gloria let out a good-natured sigh, then hurried into the next room to pull on a dry blouse and a fresh pair of jeans. Most of the time she loved her job as summer baby-sitter-in-residence at the Belvedere house on Rainbow Lake. The job meant that she could afford some new clothes for school and even contribute to her college fund. Her father's job as a postman and her mother's job as a nurse didn't offer much in the way of luxuries, and her parents were counting on her to help out with her college expenses. This summer's job might mean the difference between a decent college and something a great deal better.

But the job meant something more to Gloria. It meant living for a whole summer in the Belvedere house, a huge, stately mansion with high stone turrets that made it look like a medieval castle, perched on a cliff overlooking exclusive Rainbow Lake, one of the most glamorous resorts in the area. It meant that she could spend her mornings sitting beside the Belvederes' pool watching Mandy and Mickey play in the water and her afternoons basking in the sun on the white sand beach just below the house. She often pretended the fairy-tale castle belonged to her, that she was a princess and soon her prince would come along, recognize her as his one true love, and they would live happily ever after.

And that's what had gotten her into such a pile of trouble. That was the real problem between her and Tim O'Neal: her let's-pretend games; her fairy-tale castle; her dreams of a prince and a princess. When she thought of Tim she got all warm and fuzzy inside, just remembering the way his gray eyes lit up when he smiled and the way his brown hair curled at the nape of his neck. As far as she was concerned, she had found her prince. But when she thought of telling Tim that she wasn't the rich girl he thought she was, that warmth turned to icicles, and she shivered with a cold dread. When she had to tell him the truth, he would *know* that she wasn't a princess, just a baby-sitter from a comfortable but not rich family, pretending to be someone else.

It had all started on the beach. One Saturday, Mr. and Mrs. Belvedere had taken the twins into San Francisco, and Gloria had had the day off. She had borrowed a pair of Mrs. Belvedere's designer sunglasses, a bottle of Swedish suntan lotion, Mr. Belvedere's fancy portable radio, and a plush towel from one of the guest bathrooms and gone down to the beach. She had been lying there on her back in her brand-new bikini listening to the radio when Tim O'Neal had sat down beside her and began to talk. She had liked his confident, easy ways immediately and had been glad to hear that he and his parents would be moving to Glenwood in the fall. When she had found out that he would be a senior at Glenwood High, she had immediately invited him to Senior Orientation Weekend.

"It's one of the biggest events of the school year," she had said, rolling over to get the sun on her back. "Everybody's been looking forward to it since the end of junior year."

"I'll be glad to come if the manager will let me off,"

Tim said. "I'll have to check." He had looked apprais-ingly at her. "I don't remember seeing you before. Do you live around here?" he had asked.

That was when she had made her first mistake. It would have been so easy at that point to tell him that she was the Belvederes' baby-sitter. It would have prevented a lot of grief later. But she hadn't said a word. She had only pointed to the house on the cliff above them and said, "Up there."

Tim had whistled between his teeth. "That's a ter-rific house," he had said, looking up at it. "It looks like an old castle. What's it like living there?"

That had been her second chance. She could have said that she didn't *live* there, that she just worked there. But she hadn't. Instead she'd said, "It's great. I love it."

And that was that. From then on, Tim had thought that she was one of the Belvedere girls, a niece or a cousin, and she hadn't had the nerve to correct him. Only now she *had* to—and as soon as possible. To-day, in fact. She couldn't let him meet all her friends tomorrow thinking that she was somebody she wasn't. She had to tell him the truth, even if it meant telling him that she had lied in the first place. And pretending was every bit as bad as lying—she could see that now.

"I'm going," Gloria shouted to Mrs. Daniels, pulling a comb through her frizzy blond hair before dashing down the stairs. "I'll be back in an hour." As she jogged down the half-mile path from the Belvedere house to Rainbow Lodge, she tried to focus on the meeting and put Tim and her lie out of her mind.

"I'm sorry I'm late," Gloria said breathlessly, sliding into a chair in Mr. Dawson's office. Mr. Dawson was the recreation director at Rainbow Lodge, and they were meeting today to discuss the final details of Orientation Weekend. "I would have been on time, but just as I was about to leave the twins stuffed the kitten into the toilet, and . . ."

Ginger Goodman put a warning hand on Gloria's arm. Gloria didn't know her very well, just that Ginger had started her own catering business last year after having made a big hit with her ginger cookies. The planning committee, which Gloria chaired, had picked Ginger to provide the food at Orientation Weekend. "*Sh-h-h*," Ginger said. "Ms. Richards is going over the schedule with Mr. Dawson."

Gloria was immediately silent. Ms. Richards had been her biology teacher last year. In her classroom, you didn't dare breathe heavily, for fear of distracting her. Ms. Richards demanded your full attention from the minute you came into class until the minute you left. As the new senior adviser, she probably wasn't going to be any different. Gloria glanced at her. Ms. Richards had a list in her lap that looked as if it had about twenty items on it. Gloria sighed. No matter how well organized she tried to be, she could never in a million years manage a list with that many things to do on it.

Ms. Richards didn't exactly look like a biology teacher today. She was wearing a white cotton blouse and tan corduroy slacks, and she had her hair pulled back in a ponytail. "Senior Orientation Weekend," she was saying to Mr. Dawson, "is a very important learning experience for the students. In just a few short days, they make new friends, learn something about the outdoors, and polish their social skills. We organize it carefully to make maximum use of our learning time. About eighty of our seniors will be coming, since the weekend is optional, and many of them are still at summer jobs or away until school starts."

Mr. Dawson, a tall, rangy man with a curly brown beard and gold-rimmed glasses, stopped taking notes and looked up at her. He didn't say anything, and Ms. Richards continued to recite from her list. "The students arrive tomorrow afternoon. Tomorrow night, there will be a get-acquainted barbecue at the Wigwam, the official senior welcome, some impromptu skits, and perhaps some singing. On Friday morning, we'll take a hike around the lake, and on Friday afternoon, there will be organized games. We'll need sports equipment—for volleyball, badminton, tennis, that kind of thing." She looked up. "Are you with me?" she asked.

Mr. Dawson was writing hurriedly. "Sports equipment," he muttered, "...organized games."

"On Friday night, there will be a wiener roast on the beach."

"Do you need any special equipment for that?" Mr. Dawson joked pleasantly. The light glinted off his gold-rimmed glasses.

Ms. Richards looked up. "Pardon?"

"Nothing," Mr. Dawson muttered and went back to his notes.

"On Saturday morning, the students will attend art demonstrations and classes of their choice—pottery, drawing, painting. We'll need to use your facilities for that. On Saturday afternoon, they'll participate in organized water sports. I'd like to take a look at your sailing and wind-surfing equipment. On Saturday night, there will be a dance."

"Right," Mr. Dawson said. "To polish social skills."

Gloria smothered a giggle, and Ms. Richards's ears turned slightly pink. "Yes," she said frostily.

Mr. Dawson put down his pencil. "Will there be any time to relax and have fun?" he asked.

"Fun?" Ms. Richards replied, looking slightly

confused.

"As in throwing Frisbees on the beach, putting frogs into somebody's bunk, watching the sunset. That sort of thing."

"Well, of course there will be time for that," Ms. Richards said. She looked back at her list. She sounded a little flustered. "Although the school board is very insistent that this weekend be a learning experience for everyone . . ."

Mr. Dawson cleared his throat.

"But everyone is expected to have fun, too," she added hastily.

"I'm sure they *are*," Mr. Dawson said in a dry voice. "*Expected* to, that is." He turned to Ginger. "Are you the young lady who's providing the food?"

Ginger nodded, trying not to laugh. "Everything is taken care of," she said, with a confident wave of her hand. "My assistant, Craig Stevenson, is bringing up the rest of the supplies today, and we're all set to get to work for tomorrow night's barbecue."

"It's a little unusual for the lodge to permit a group to bring in an outside caterer," Mr. Dawson said. "But because you were a senior last year, they've made an exception." He grinned. "How does it feel to be an old senior?"

Ginger pouted. "Do you have to put it that way?" she asked. "Wouldn't 'graduated senior' do just as well?"

Mr. Dawson laughed and turned to face Gloria. "Don't I know you from somewhere?"

Gloria blushed and looked at her feet. They *did* know each other. "Don't you remember last week?" she asked. "You helped me get Mickey down from the cliff."

Mr. Dawson leaned back in his chair. "Oh, right," he said with a smile. "I'll bet you've had your hands full taking care of those two all summer."

Gloria laughed. "You can say that again."

Ms. Richards cleared her throat and said coolly, "I think, if you have no objection, that we'd better take a tour of the camp now. I have to get back to Glenwood this afternoon."

Mr. Dawson stood up and reached for the battered brown cowboy hat that hung beside his desk. "Sure, let's go. Everybody follow me."

"Isn't that interesting?" Ginger said under her breath to Gloria as they followed Mr. Dawson and Ms. Richards across the lodge grounds.

"What?" Gloria asked. She was thinking about Tim. She had caught a glimpse of him in the dining room as they left Mr. Dawson's office. Seeing him reminded her of what she had to do today, and she could feel the icicles inside her forming a giant iceberg. How was she ever going to tell him?

"Mr. Dawson and Ms. Richards. Don't you think they make a cute couple?"

Gloria shivered. "I don't think Ms. Richards would make a cute couple with *anybody*," she said. "Have you ever had her?"

Ginger shook her head. "I had Smothers for biology. Is she tough?"

"Dragon Lady," Gloria said, as they came to a stop behind Mr. Dawson and Ms. Richards. They were standing in front of a group of small log cabins.

"These are the girls' bunkhouses," Mr. Dawson was saying. "Each bunk sleeps eight or ten girls." The cabins had screened-in windows on all four sides and roll-up canvas awnings to keep out the rain. He gestured toward the creek. "The boys' bunks are over there, about fifty yards on the other side of Cypress Creek."

"Good," Ms. Richards said, with a note of satisfaction in her voice. "That will cut down on the amount of after-hours traffic."

"I wouldn't bet on it," Ginger whispered. "A little creek isn't going to keep the guys away from the girls. I bet they'd even swim the lake if they had to."

Ms. Richards overheard. "Ginger, you don't *really* think that, do you?" she asked.

"Of course I do." Ginger laughed. "If you want to

know who's been visiting after-hours, just look for the guys with wet feet."

Ms. Richards pulled out her list. "We've already selected our bunk supervisors," she said worriedly, "but maybe we'd better add another one or two, just to be on the safe side."

Mr. Dawson laughed. "I wouldn't bother if I were you," he said teasingly. "A little after-hours traffic never hurt anybody. Anyway, what would a few days at camp be like if a few boys didn't show up for some after-midnight harassment of the girls?" He winked at her. "Who knows? It might even be fun, Dana."

Ms. Richards stiffened. She glanced at her watch. It didn't look to Gloria as if she thought that would be fun at all. "Gloria, tomorrow morning, will you check all the bunks to be sure that the linens are in order?"

"Yes, ma'am," Gloria said dutifully. She leaned toward Ginger. "Do you have a pencil and piece of paper?" she whispered. "I need to make a list."

"A list for just one thing?" Ginger asked incredulously, handing over a pencil and a scrap of chewing-gum wrapper.

"I have a terrible memory," Gloria confessed. "I lose things if I don't write down where I've put them."

Ms. Richards turned back to Mr. Dawson. "Really,

I think we'd better hurry. I have to get back to the . . ."

Mr. Dawson reached for her hand. "Well, then, come on," he said. "Let's hurry." And he pulled her along the path toward the boathouse. "You *do* have time to check out the sailing equipment before you go, don't you?"

Ginger and Gloria trailed behind. "There, didn't I tell you?" Ginger said triumphantly. "They make a really cute couple. I predict that something is going to happen between them this weekend." She grinned. "Wouldn't that be great?"

Gloria stumbled over a rock. "Yeah, great," she said absently, her thoughts already drifting back to Tim.

"Hi," Gloria said. She'd been sitting on the lodge deck for the last half hour, watching the twilight fall across the lake and waiting for Tim to finish his shift in the dining room.

"Hi," Tim said, as he slipped onto the bench beside her. He loosened his tie and put his feet up on the deck rail. She could see that his black oxfords were polished to a shine to match the crisply pressed black slacks and white shirt of his waiter's uniform.

"Hard day in the dining room?" Gloria asked with a little laugh.

Tim winced. "I must've walked miles today," he

said. "How about you? Hard day at the beach? Or did you spend the day at the pool?" He reached for her hand with a smile. "You must be tired from all that strenuous relaxation."

Gloria pulled her hand back, feeling her face burn. Tim had a way of getting right to the heart of the matter. If only he knew that wasn't the kind of life she led. How was she ever going to find the courage to tell him the truth? What a mess. And, as usual, she had no one to blame but herself.

"Oh, I did a lot today," she said, shrugging. "Ginger Goodman and I had a meeting with Ms. Richards and Mr. Dawson about Senior Orientation Weekend. You know, planning, getting things ready, stuff like that." She glanced at him. "Did you find out if you can come?"

Tim shrugged. "I still don't know if I can get off work," he said. "We're shorthanded in the dining room." He grinned teasingly. "But I'm glad you did something useful today," he said. "That's better than lazing around on the beach all afternoon." He ducked the light slap that Gloria aimed at him and caught her hand and held it. "How about doing something useful tonight . . . like sitting on the beach beside a fire, watching the moon come up. We might even roast a hot dog or two."

"Sounds wonderful," Gloria said.

"Oh, Gloria," Tim added, "my folks are coming up tomorrow. I want you to meet them. Think there'll be time?"

Gloria nodded. His parents! She was going to meet his parents! "I guess so," she said slowly.

"Gosh, you sound enthusiastic," Tim teased. "They know the Belvederes. They'll be interested in meeting you, I know."

"I'd like to meet them, too," she said, trying to sound as if it were the truth. Now she really *would* have to tell him tonight. It would be her last chance. She wanted him to know she wasn't a Belvedere before he introduced her to his parents. And anyway, tomorrow all her friends would arrive, and she couldn't risk his learning the truth from one of them. He would never forgive her.

The evening on the beach was wonderful. While Tim's portable radio played softly in the background, they built a driftwood fire and snuggled together on a blanket, eating hot dogs and marshmallows and watching the golden flames lick at the shadows. Gloria kept looking for a chance to ease into the subject that was most on her mind—the truth about her identity—but the opportunity just didn't seem to present itself. She and Tim didn't talk much; and when the moon finally rose and hung like a fat white lantern over the lake, Tim took her in his arms, and they stopped talking altogether.

When Tim walked her back to the Belvedere house and kissed her good night, she realized that their evening together was over and she still hadn't told him the truth. The moon over the lake, the soft breeze, and Tim's gentle good-night kiss seemed to have cast a spell over her, and she couldn't bring herself to break it.

"Tomorrow," she promised herself, as she drifted off to sleep. "I'll tell him tomorrow... before the buses arrive... before his parents come."

Chapter Two

Angela Maroni stood in front of the bathroom mirror in the cramped little bathroom, humming the melody from a Bruce Springsteen song under her breath and staring at her reflection in the water-spotted glass. Out in the living room, her two younger sisters were noisily debating which soap opera to watch. In the kitchen, her mother was yelling at Angie's little nephew for stealing a pocketful of cookies, and in the driveway, just under the bathroom window, her older brother Tony was angrily pounding the latest dent out of the fender of his red GTO. Angie felt like putting her fingers in her ears to shut out the racket, but there wasn't time to stand around with her fingers in her ears. If she didn't put on her makeup and finish packing in the next half hour, Tony was going to take off without her. And then she would miss the bus—and missing the bus would mean missing Orientation Weekend up at Rainbow Lake.

Missing Orientation Weekend was simply unthinkable. She had been looking forward to this all summer long, dreaming fairy-tale dreams and fantasizing about the amazing things that were going to happen there. After all, she reminded herself, it *was* the beginning of her senior year, the most important year of her life so far. This weekend was going to be a wonderful, magical time, Angie thought, carefully applying eye liner to the corners of her dark eyes, to emphasize their almond shape. She had always had a job after school, and she hadn't been very involved in school activities in the past couple of years. But she was going to change all that now. This weekend she hoped to make lots of new friends, find people who would appreciate her as a special and worthwhile person in her own right—and maybe even attract Glenn St. Clair's attention. It was a terrific dream. Even if it was only a dream. Her chances of attracting Glenn St. Clair were probably one in a million.

Angie smudged the line at the corner of her right eye, wiped it off with her fingertip, and tried again. Try as she might to be casual about him, that's what always happened when she thought of Glenn St. Clair. Her hands started to tremble, her stomach filled with fluttery butterflies, and a nervous knot formed in her throat. Glenn had had that effect on her ever since spring semester, when he first sat across from her in Ms. Richards's biology lab. At first she had thought it was just a crush, but now, after trying unsuccessfully to push him out of her mind all summer, she wasn't so sure that it *was* just a crush. Didn't crushes come and go in a matter of days, or a month or so? Well, this one had come, but it hadn't gone away, even after six months, so maybe it was more than a crush.

She stopped singing and began to put on her lipstick—a bright orangy lipstick that made her mouth look full and sexy and ready to be kissed, the way women looked in the magazines that Tony kept under his bed. If only she could get Glenn to want to *know* her, really know her—not the Angie that everybody else knew, the Angie whose father had been sent to prison for stealing cars, and whose brother was on parole for shoplifting... Not the Angie who talked tough and acted tough because that's the way the street kids in North Glenwood talked and acted... and certainly not the Angie who never had any real friends, because the kids she admired and most wanted to be like were too worried about their own reputations to risk being around her long enough to find out what she was really like. She had this crazy feeling that even though Glenn was last year's junior-class president and a sure bet for president of the student body this year, he was the kind of person who might be willing to take that risk.

"Hey, Angie!" The doorknob rattled, and Tony's harsh voice interrupted her thoughts. "If you don't move it out in a hurry, kid, you ain't gonna be movin' out at all. I gotta be at work in fifteen minutes."

"Tony, I'm not ready!" Angie wailed, dropping the tube of lipstick into the sink. "You said I had another half hour! I haven't even finished packing yet!"

The doorknob rattled again. "Well, that's the way it is. If you want a ride, you got five minutes."

Hastily, Angie scrambled her makeup into a plastic bag. She had wanted a real makeup kit, the pretty kind that folded over neatly and held everything in clever little compartments, but she hadn't been able to afford it. When the Maroni kids worked, Mrs. Maroni made it clear that she expected them to contribute to the grocery money. Angie had been lucky to clear enough from her paycheck at Louie's Delicatessen, where she had worked most of the summer, to buy some new clothes for school and a new pair of shorts for Senior Orientation Weekend. There hadn't been anything left over to squander on a makeup kit.

"Hang on, kid," Tony shouted, revving the engine of his GTO as he turned into the parking lot. "Let's give 'em something to gawk at."

Something to gawk at! Angie thought. That was all she needed. As if Tony's car weren't enough for them to gawk at with its jacked-up rear end, orange flames curling wickedly down both sides, a dragon painted on the hood, and a license plate that advertised the whole thing as HOT STUFF. "Listen, Tony," she said urgently, grabbing his arm. "Just stop here and let me get out. You don't need to drive all the way through the lot."

"And make you walk in this heat?" Tony asked, shaking off her hand. "Nothing doin'. What's the matter? You afraid to have your hotshot friends see you ridin' in style? Hang on!" He shifted and popped the clutch, and the tires squealed painfully.

Angie's face flushed, and she slid partway down in the seat. "Tony, I wish you wouldn't," she whispered, hanging on to the armrest as Tony wrestled the wheel around. "Please let me out."

"Hey, Angie, just relax," Tony said, grinning, weaving crazily through the neat rows of parked Hondas and Mazdas. "I'm givin' you something to live up to."

Angie slid farther down in the seat, her face burning, her heart racing. Everybody knew about her father's prison sentence and Tony's parole. Now they would think that she was nothing but a low-rider besides. Didn't they have enough to gossip about and make fun of already? "Something to live *down*, you mean." She gritted her teeth.

"Okay, kid, we're here," Tony said, slamming on the brakes and screeching to a stop alongside the buses, in front of a gang of kids. "Get out." He jerked the transmission into neutral and revved the engine again.

Angie pulled her duffel bag from the backseat and reached for the door handle.

"Not that way," Tony said.

"What way, then?" Angie asked, bewildered.

Tony jerked his thumb with a toothy grin. "The window," he said. "You got to climb out the window. I ain't got around to fixin' the door yet. The handle's broke. That's why I told you to get in my side when we left the house."

Angie's eyes grew round. "The *window*?" she said. "Tony, I *can't* climb out of the window! Not in front of everybody!"

"Whadd'ya mean, you can't climb out the window?" he growled. "My friends do it all the time. It's easy. You just stick your leg out and then hoist the rest through. No sweat."

Angie shook her head, the tears welling hotly in her eyes and threatening to slide onto her cheeks. "I can't," she whispered. "Please let me out your side, Tony. Please."

Tony shook his head stubbornly and put the car into gear. "I ain't gettin' out," he said. "I'm late already. So I guess you're comin' to work with me." The car rocked forward. "It's just as well. You didn't want to go to that stupid lake with those stupid rich kids anyhow."

"Stop!" Angie screamed, dumping her duffel bag out the window. "I'll do it!" As Tony stopped, she took a deep breath and put one bare, tanned leg out the window. Just at that moment, she heard a shriek of laughter.

"God, I can't believe it," a girl's voice cried in shrill amusement. "Look, everybody! It's Angie Maroni, climbing out a car window!"

Angie threw an anguished glanced in the direction of the voice and saw Shannon Welles, blond and dainty in a pair of crisp white shorts and a pink white ruffled top, pointing at her. Angie hesitated, balanced half in and half out the window, feeling so humiliated that she wanted to die.

"Come on, kid, hurry up," Tony snapped. "I ain't got all day." The car began to inch forward again. "Get out if you're gettin' out."

"Here, let me help," a voice said. Angie felt a pair of strong hands around her waist. "Just relax. I've got you." Angie recognized the voice immediately. It was Glenn St. Clair!

The shock of feeling Glenn's hands on her was so great that Angie suddenly lost her balance and tumbled backward into his arms, nearly knocking him into the side of the bus. Tony's GTO roared away with a screech of rubber and a spray of dust and pebbles.

"Oh, I'm sorry," she whispered, the flush spreading from her cheeks to her throat. "I...I...didn't mean to..."

Glenn was leaning against the bus, both hands still on her hips. "You okay?" he asked. There was a mischievous gleam in his green eyes. He dropped his hands slowly, as Angie nodded. "Do you always do things the hard way?"

Angie pulled herself up. Was Glenn making fun of her? "What other way is there?" she said in a brittle voice. She swallowed, trying to smile. "Actually, my specialty is climbing out of sun roofs. Windows are too easy."

Glenn grinned and chuckled softly. "Well, I'm curious to see how you handle getting out of the window of this bus," he said, pointing over his shoulder with his thumb. "That ought to be a real challenge, even for somebody who specializes in sun roofs."

Shannon sauntered over. Possessively, she tucked her hand through Glenn's arm. "Glenn," she said, her blue eyes narrowing as she glanced at Angie, "Carl's here. He's got something important he wants to talk to you about." She tugged at his arm. "Come *on*."

"Well, thanks," Angie said, stepping back awkwardly. She bit her lip.

"Don't mention it," Glenn said with a smile, as he turned away. "Anytime you feel like climbing out a window, let me know."

Over her shoulder, Shannon threw Angie an icy glare. "Really, Glenn," she said, just loud enough for Angie to hear, "don't you know about the Maronis? She's got a terrible reputation. You don't want to be seen hanging around with her."

Angie's heart sank into her tennis shoes. How could she ever compete with someone as pretty and cool and self-assured as Shannon Welles? It was impossible. And the sooner she faced up to facts, the better.

Picking up her duffel bag, Angie went straight to the bus and took a seat at the very back, where it wouldn't be so noticeable when nobody sat beside her. As the kids got on, she sank lower and lower into the seat, pretending to look out the window. There were couples, girl and boy, arms around each other. There were groups, three and four together, laughing, teasing, hugging. Angie had never felt so alone in all her life.

"Anybody sitting here?"

Angie looked up. A slim, dark-haired girl wearing jeans and a Glenwood High sweat shirt was standing next to her. She looked vaguely familiar. Angie half-nodded, hoping the girl would get discouraged and sit somewhere else.

"Look, it's the only seat left on the bus," the girl said with a shrug, "and the other bus is already full. Either I sit here or I hitchhike up to the lake. What'll it be?"

Angie moved toward the window without saying anything. The bus lurched once and started off.

"Thanks," the girl said, tossing her bag into the overhead rack and getting comfortable in the seat beside Angie. "My name is Stephanie. Stephanie Burroughs."

"Angela," Angie said. "Angie Maroni." She eyed Stephanie for a moment, then asked, "Weren't you a senior last year?"

"Yeah, that's right," Stephanie said, stretching her legs under the seat ahead of her and yawning. "I'm doing double time."

Angie considered that for a minute in silence. "Really?" she asked at last. "How come you're doing that? It's not because you just *felt* like having two senior years, is it?"

Stephanie laughed. "Hardly," she said. "There was a lot about last year I *didn't* like. Some of the sorority stuff, for instance, and the stuck-up kids who always seem to think that they're better than anybody else."

"Well, then," Angie asked, suddenly curious to know more, "why did you come back?"

"Because I want to go to a good college," Stephanie said, matter-of-factly, "and my school record has so many holes in it, it looks like a piece of Swiss cheese. I moved around a lot as a kid, and most of the time I didn't care whether or not I did okay in school. It wasn't until I got to Glenwood last year that I began to settle down and try to do well. I didn't particularly want to repeat senior year, but it seems like the best thing to do."

Angie began to feel more comfortable than she had felt all day. Stephanie could have given her some long-winded explanation about *wanting* to repeat the year. But she hadn't. She'd said exactly what she felt. "Well," Angie said slowly, not looking at Stephanie, "It must take a lot of guts to repeat a year. It sounds like you don't care too much what people think." *Not like me,* she added silently to herself.

Stephanie grinned broadly. "That's me," she said. "I get in trouble sometimes for not saying what people want to hear. I always figure that people are going to think whatever they want to, no matter what I say. I know I can't change the way people think, so I don't try."

Angie propped her legs up against the seat in front of her and settled back. "Tell me what senior year is like," she said.

"Sure," Stephanie began. "There's nothing I like better than talking." For the next half hour, she told Angie about everything that had happened during her first senior year, the football games, the basketball tournament, the parties and dances, the friends she had made. "I guess that's what I'm going to miss the most," she said slowly. "My friends. It's not going to seem like senior year without them."

Friends, Angie thought. It would be nice to have friends—friends who accepted you for what *you* were, not for what they thought your father or your brother were—friends who would stand by you, no matter what.

"...Like my sister," Stephanie was saying. "I mean, my foster sister, Alex Enomoto. She was my best friend. She left for Northwestern last week to study diving under this famous Olympic diving coach. I'm really going to miss her. We had a great summer together, though. Before she left for school, we spent six weeks in Japan, with her father." She giggled. "You should have seen us, Angie. It was a riot. One night, Alex got dressed up like a geisha girl in a silk kimono and obi and slippers, and she sneaked into this geisha place. She really had people believing she was one of them. It was classic." She smiled. "But that's crazy Alex. It's going to be hard to get through this year without her." She turned to face Angie. "You know, I guess that was the best part of senior year, when you get right down to it. The parties and games and dances and stuff, those are just things you *do*. Your friends are the really important part."

Suddenly, the weekend ahead didn't seem quite so bleak to Angie. She had already made one friend who seemed to share a lot of her feelings. And where there was one, there were bound to be others. She sat up straighter and looked around the bus, seeing several girls she recognized and thinking how nice it would be to end the weekend with two or three good friends.

And there was still the possibility that she would get to know Glenn St. Clair. After all, she had dreamed all summer that this was going to be a magical weekend. Who could say what improbable things might happen? She blushed when she remembered the feel of his warm hands around her waist and his smile, just before Shannon dragged him off. It had seemed like such a genuine smile.

Suddenly Angie noticed Shannon and Glenn several seats in front of her. Shannon was leaning toward Glenn, her smooth blond hair swinging against his cheek, her hand, with its scarlet-painted nails, resting possessively on his shoulder. It was as clear as day, Angie thought despairingly. Glenn belonged to Shannon, and she wasn't about to let him go.

Angie slumped back down in the seat. Even if it weren't for Shannon, she thought sadly, how could I ever expect someone as nice and *respectable* as Glenn St. Clair to get involved with someone like me? Everybody knows about the trouble my family's been in. And some people, like Shannon, think a bad reputation is contagious.

Chapter Three

When Gloria got up on Thursday morning, she looked at herself in the mirror and held up three fingers, Girl Scout style. "I swear," she said fervently, "to tell him the truth and nothing but the truth. So help me God. I'm going to confess. Today."

The Belvederes had given her the weekend off, so Gloria didn't have to worry about the twins today. The sun hadn't broken through the early-morning fog yet, and the air was still chilly, so she pulled on a sweater and went down the path toward the lodge, carrying a small suitcase and her overnight bag. She would be staying in the camp with the others for the whole weekend.

Today was going to be really exciting, she thought to herself, after she confessed to Tim and got that awful task off her mind. Of course, she knew why she had been putting it off. It was out of fear that Tim wouldn't be interested in her if he knew she wasn't from a wealthy, prominent family. She knew he had strong feelings for her, but would he feel differently if he knew she had deceived him? Well, there was only one way to find out, and she couldn't put it off any longer. She had to tell him before he introduced her to his parents. Since they knew the Belvederes, they would know immediately that she wasn't a member of the Belvedere family. No matter how unpleasant it was going to be, she *had* to tell him today.

At least there were other more pleasant things to look forward to. She was especially anxious to see Nancy Colton, her best friend from junior year. Nancy had been visiting her grandparents in San Diego during the summer, and while they had exchanged the usual wish-you-were-here postcards and a few letters, Gloria had a lot to tell Nancy—mostly about Tim. She would understand how Gloria had gotten herself into this mess. Nancy had a vivid imagination and wanted to be a writer. In fact, she was writing a novel right now—a love story. Gloria smiled to herself. *Her* love story was more complicated than any novel she had ever read. Maybe Nancy could use it as part of her plot.

But before Gloria got sidetracked thinking about

seeing Nancy and all her other friends, she had to find Tim. They had agreed to get together at four that afternoon, when he would introduce her to his parents. She had between now and four to make her confession.

"Have you seen Tim this morning?" she asked Carole, one of the girls who worked with him in the dining room.

"He's off today," Carole said, straightening a pile of napkins. "I hear that his parents are here for the weekend."

With a feeling of panic, Gloria looked around. Suddenly she realized that she didn't even know where Tim lived. The time they spent together had been at the lodge or on the beach. Why hadn't she thought of getting an address or a phone number from him?

As Carole picked up a stack of plates and turned to go into the kitchen, Gloria said, "If you see him, tell him I'd really like to talk to him. It's . . . kind of important."

"Oh, there you are, Gloria," Ms. Richards said as she entered the dining room. "Have you checked the bunks yet for linens and bedding?"

Gloria shook her head. "I forgot my list," she said. It was true. She had stuck the gum wrapper into the pocket of yesterday's jeans and had forgotten all about checking the bunks. "Anyway," she added, "I have to find this friend of mine. I've got something that's really kind of urgent to tell him."

Ms. Richards frowned. "Well, perhaps you could take care of the bunks first," she said. "That's really kind of urgent, too, you know. The buses will be arriving right after noon, and you won't have a chance to take care of it once everyone's here."

Gloria sighed. "Yes, ma'am," she said. Well, it wouldn't take long, and maybe Tim would show up by the time she was finished.

It took Gloria almost two hours to go through all the cabins on both sides of Cypress Creek, checking for missing pillows, blankets, sheets, and towels. After several trips back to the lodge for replacements, she finally finished her work and ran to the dining room.

"Have you seen Tim yet?" she asked Carole, who was settling a bowl of lettuce into the salad bar.

"Nope." Carole shook her head. "Listen, why don't you ask the manager, Gloria? I'll bet he knows where the O'Neals stay when they're here."

"Why should *he* know where Tim's parents are staying?" Gloria asked, puzzled.

Carole looked at her oddly for a minute, then turned away. "I'll tell him you're looking for him if I happen to run into him," she said and went back to her work.

"Hey, Gloria!" Ginger waved to her from across the room. She had on a pair of bright green jogging shorts, and with her reddish-brown hair, lots of heads turned to look at her as she headed toward Gloria. "Craig and I are ready to put up the welcome banner. Want to help? The buses will be here pretty soon."

"I guess so," Gloria said with a sigh, looking at her watch. There was no point in looking for Tim. She didn't even know where to start. For all she knew, he could be staying with his parents at a motel in town. If she was outside working, she could keep an eye out for him.

The welcome banner was a big white sheet on which Ginger and Gloria had painted WELCOME SENIORS! in bright red letters. With Craig's help, they were stringing it between two tall pine trees in front of the lodge.

"I can't wait for everyone to get here," Ginger said, as she and Gloria held the ladder for Craig. "I haven't seen Stephanie Burroughs all summer. She's coming as a repeat senior and a bunk supervisor. And Ms. Richards told me Elaine Gregory is going to be a bunk supervisor, too." Ginger smiled. "You know, it's going to seem like a class reunion with the three of us here together."

"And Bernie Kaufman and Chuck Hadley are coming to supervise the boys," Gloria said. Both of the boys had been seniors the year before. Chuck had won a scholarship to Stanford, and Bernie was studying photography in San Francisco. Gloria didn't know either of them very well.

"Oh, God. Remember Grad Night, Craig?" Ginger asked as he climbed down the ladder. "Is Chuck still going with Cheryl Abrahamson?"

The three of them moved the ladder to the other tree. "How could I ever forget it?" Craig said, starting up the ladder again. "One minute Cheryl was all decked out like a movie star, sexy clothes, lots of makeup, and the next she looked like a drowned rat, with mascara running down both cheeks."

"We went to Disneyland for Grad Night," Ginger explained to Gloria, "and on the Pirates of the Caribbean ride, Cheryl fell overboard, and Chuck had to dive in and fish her out. It was pretty funny, but I couldn't help feeling sort of bad for her, if you know what I mean."

Gloria nodded.

"Well, anyway," Craig said, coming back down the ladder, "it will be good to see Chuck again. He's okay. Bernie, too." He paused. "Hey, I didn't tell you about last night, did I?"

"What happened?" Ginger asked.

Craig motioned for Ginger and Gloria to take one end of the ladder. He picked up the other end, and they started toward the tool shed. "Ms. Richards called me from Glenwood and said she'd been thinking about what she called the 'bunk situation.' She asked if I'd sleep on the boys' side and help Bernie and Chuck supervise." He glanced back over his shoulder, a puzzled look on his face. "She said something about watching for wet feet."

Gloria and Ginger dropped their end of the ladder and began to giggle, and in a minute they were rolling on the grass, howling with laughter. Craig looked at them, puzzled. "Did I say something funny?" he asked.

"Funny?" Ginger gasped, trying to sit up. "Oh, no, not at all."

"Just keep your feet dry, Craig, that's all," Gloria said, catching her breath. "Ms. Richards plans a foot inspection every morning at seven-thirty." The two girls burst into laughter again.

By the time they had let Craig in on the joke and calmed down enough to put the ladder away, the buses had arrived. The three of them lined up in the driveway in front of the lodge, waving and smiling as the kids began to spill out into the parking lot.

"There's Nancy!" Gloria dashed through the crowd and flung her arms around Nancy's neck.

"Oh, Nancy," she cried, "I'm so glad to see you!" She hugged her hard. "You've cut your hair! It looks cute!" Nancy was petite and lively, and her new chin-length haircut gave her an almost elfin look.

"Gloria!" Nancy exclaimed, holding her friend at arm's length so she could look at her. "You look terrific! You're so tan! You must have spent *hours* lying on the beach. Tell me about your summer. Did you meet any boys?"

"Only one," Gloria said. "But I *do* have a lot to tell you about him." She heaved a dramatic sigh. "His name is Tim."

Nancy gave her a long, searching look. "Oh, my God," she said, with a horrified expression. "You're in love, aren't you?"

Gloria laughed a little uncomfortably. "I guess so," she said. "Yes, I guess that's what you'd call it." She looked at Nancy. "You make it sound like I've got a bad case of poison ivy or something."

"Well, that's what it's like—" Nancy sighed—"poison ivy. It itches and you can't scratch it. In fact, there isn't *anything* you can do, except try to live through it. Anyway, I know that I've had it as far as love is concerned. I'm serious. Never again."

"Uh-oh," Gloria said softly. "What happened?"

"Well, I met a great guy in San Diego. We did everything together all summer long, and...well, he seemed just about perfect. I thought he was starting to love me." Nancy swallowed hard, and Gloria saw a tear forming at the corner of her eye. "But then I found out just last week that he's got this steady girl friend that he's really serious about. She was away for the summer, and I was just a replacement, like in the theater—a summer stand-in when the star's on vacation."

Gloria put her arm around Nancy's shoulders. "Oh, Nancy, I'm so sorry," she said softly. "That's pretty awful."

Nancy put her face against Gloria's shoulder. "I don't think I'll ever love anybody again," she said in a muffled voice. "Not ever."

Gloria shivered. Would she feel like that if things didn't work out between her and Tim? They were just getting to know each other, and everything seemed so right when they were together. But Tim was so honest and straightforward, and a lie would be a hard thing for him to swallow. Maybe in a few hours, after she'd told Tim the truth, she'd be feeling the way Nancy was feeling.

But she didn't have time to think about it then. The empty buses had pulled away, and everybody was busy catching up on the summer's news and waiting for directions to their cabins.

In a few minutes, the new seniors were all seated in

a semicircle on the ground in front of the steps, listening for their bunk assignments. Ms. Richards introduced Mr. Dawson, and then the supervisors—Chuck, Bernie, and Craig for the boys and Stephanie and Elaine for the girls. They spoke briefly about themselves as they were introduced. Ginger would also be available to help with the girls, Ms. Richards told them, although dealing with the food was going to take up a lot of her time during the weekend. "For your information," she added, "the boys' bunks are located across Cypress Creek"—she paused emphatically—"quite a distance from the girls' bunks."

A loud groan of disapproval swept through the group, and Mr. Dawson grinned. "Hey," one of the guys spoke up, "I thought this was an equal-opportunity camp! How can we have equal opportunity if the boys and girls are separated?"

Ginger was sitting on the porch rail listening. "Hey, listen, no sweat," she said. "There'll be plenty of equal opportunities—on the beach, in the woods, out on the lake. But separating boys' and girls' bunks is sort of like separating the egg yolk from the egg white. That way you'll be sure that nothing gets hatched." Ginger's joke turned the groans to instant laughter, and the group broke up and started toward the cabins, still laughing.

Gloria discovered that she had been assigned to one of the smaller cabins, along with Nancy, Angie Maroni, Rayne Ramirez, and a girl she didn't know named Lani Connors. Stephanie Burroughs would be their bunk supervisor. She didn't know Stephanie well, but she liked the matter-of-fact way she had described herself when she was introduced.

"Hey, this is okay," Nancy said, plopping her suitcase down on one of the lower bunks. She looked at the screened-in windows. "But doesn't it get a little damp when it rains?"

Gloria laughed. "All we have to do is roll down the canvas awning," she said, climbing onto the bunk above Nancy's. She began to unpack her overnight case and put her things on the small shelf beside her bed.

"Hey, everybody, I'm here!" A thin girl with long, dark hair and a lean, intelligent-looking face stood in the doorway.

"Who are you?" Gloria asked curiously, peering over the edge of the bunk.

"I'm Lani Connors," the girl announced, putting her bag on the opposite bunk.

"I know a Marcia Connors," Nancy said, "but I don't suppose..."

"That's what everybody says," Lani said dejectedly, slumping onto the edge of the bunk and propping her chin in her hands. "Everybody looks at us and says that we can't *possibly* be sisters."

"You're Marcia Connors's *sister*?" Gloria said, with genuine surprise. Marcia had been the most beautiful girl in last year's senior class. How could this plain, awkward girl be Marcia's sister? And if she had been a junior last year, why hadn't they met before?

"Right," Lani sighed. She sat up straight and made a face. "That's who I am. Marcia Connors's freaky, plain little sister."

"Freaky?" Nancy said.

Lani shrugged. "Well, I don't know what *you'd* call it, but I'd call it freaky. After all, when you've been sentenced to special schools all your life . . ."

"Special schools?" Gloria asked.

"Schools for the gifted, that's what they call them." She pulled her knees up and sat cross-legged on the bed. "You know, where everybody does quantum physics and computer programming for fun and watches Shakespeare on television even when it's not assigned." She brightened. "But this year's going to be different. I finally managed to talk my parents into letting me go to a *real* school for my senior year, with normal kids, instead of freaky kids." She spread out her arms, grinning broadly. "So I'm here, everybody! I'm here!"

"Hooray for Lani!" Nancy called out from the bottom bunk, "joining the normal kids at last. So what's Marcia up to?" she asked, leaning forward. "She was in Drama Club with me last fall. She's so gorgeous, I always thought she'd end up as an actress in Hollywood—or maybe as a model in New York."

Lani shook her head. "Nope, guess again," she said proudly. "Marcia's studying nursing."

Nancy shook her head, mystified. "Well, she'll be the most beautiful nurse around. But I'm surprised that she'd want to be a nurse. She had such a reputation for..."

Just then the cabin door opened. A slender, brown-haired girl with a waiflike look about her was standing in the doorway, watching them with an expression halfway between fear and defiance.

"Angie," Gloria said quietly, wishing that Nancy's last word hadn't been *reputation*. What if Angie thought they had been talking about her? "Hi. Hey, everybody, this is Angie Maroni." She tried to think of something else to say. "Angie was in my music class last semester," she added, after an uncomfortable pause. "She's got a great voice." Well, that was true. Angie really could sing.

Hesitantly, almost fearfully, Angie stepped forward through a chorus of hellos. Gloria slid down from her bunk. She didn't know Angie very well, but she knew *about* her. Everybody did. Poor Angie. It must be awful to have everyone whispering behind your back all the time, speculating about you. Still, looking at her, it was hard to believe that she could be as bad as some of the kids said. Gloria knew Angie's father was in jail and her older brother was out on parole for shoplifting, but that didn't have anything to do with Angie. Just because a few people in her family had made mistakes, it didn't mean that *Angie* was bad.

"Hey, Angie, how about this bunk?" Gloria said, trying to sound offhand about it. She gestured toward the best bunk in the room, against the back wall.

For a minute Angie stared at her suspiciously. Then she offered a shy smile and dropped her duffel bag on the bed.

Nancy cleared her throat. "Lani was just telling us that she was in a school for the gifted last year, Angie."

"It was a school for freaks," Lani said. The word *freaks* dropped like a stone into the middle of the silence, and Gloria could sense Angie tensing up like a hurt animal.

"'Freaks' as in abnormally intelligent kids," Gloria explained, as she sat down next to Angie.

"Lani is going to a regular school for the first time in her life."

Angie looked up, her brown eyes enormous in a circle of eye shadow, her too-orange lipstick smeared a little at the corners of her mouth. "Well, welcome to Glenwood, Lani," she said softly. "I hope you make lots of friends."

Lani sighed. "So do I," she said. "That's something I'm not very good at, I'm afraid. And I want to change." She looked sad. "It seems like once people know about my background and realize I have a brain, they don't want to have anything to do with me. I guess it scares them."

Angie looked sympathetic. "I can understand that," she said. "Some people have trouble with anybody who's different from them."

Lani waved her hand. "Yeah, and boys are the worst," she said. "My sister, Marcia, was a whiz at boys. But it didn't rub off on me." She looked around at the others. "But I'm going to change all that, and soon. I have this great new project that will help me find the perfect boyfriend. I've decided to interview all the boys and find out what they think about girls and love, and in the meantime, I'll be collecting all sorts of information on what makes a boyfriend perfect."

"Nothing makes a boyfriend perfect," a new voice

announced, from the door. "In fact, there is no such thing as the perfect boyfriend. He doesn't exist."

"Amen!" Nancy said fervently.

"Rayne!" Gloria cried, leaping up. "Oh, I'm so glad to see you!"

Rayne Ramirez was tall and willowy and absolutely gorgeous, with deep-set dark eyes and thick, wavy brown hair. She had been born in Mexico City, and she was a real Latin beauty. She was the new head cheerleader of the Glennettes. Cheryl Abrahamson had handed over her pompoms to Rayne in a tearful ceremony at the end of the school year, with everyone applauding.

Lani looked at her curiously. "If you'll pardon my saying so," she said, "it doesn't look to me like *you'd* have any trouble with boys."

Rayne put her bag at the foot of the cot by the door. "No, but I know enough to know none of them are perfect. Most of them are just plain thickheaded. They don't even *want* to understand anything about true friendship. They don't know anything about loyalty or about standing by somebody who needs them." Her dark eyes glinted with anger, and Nancy wondered if she was talking about any boy in particular.

"Does anybody?" Angie asked, staring at her intently. "I mean, does anybody really understand what true friendship is?"

"Let's hope so," Gloria said, looking at Angie's face. Her question seemed so poignant and sad.

Lani sighed. "Well, that's what this weekend's supposed to be about, isn't it?" she asked. "Friendship? That's what the letter from the school board said, anyway. I quote: 'Senior Orientation Weekend is designed to foster friendship and encourage students to enhance their social skills in a natural setting.' Unquote."

Gloria put her arm around Angie's shoulder and said, "Well, I think we're all on our way to finding new friends."

Angie's smile made Gloria feel better than she had all week.

"Yeah, well, friendship is all well and good," Lani said, dumping the contents of a book bag on her bed. "But I plan to spend lots of time this weekend researching boys. And the sooner I start, the better." She looked around. "Does anybody know what time we eat? I want to start my project before dinner."

Gloria glanced at her watch. "It's nearly four," she reported. Nearly four! She jumped up. "Oh, no," she gasped. "I promised Tim I'd meet him at four. And I have to talk to him... have to tell him..." She grabbed her red sweater from the bunk and headed for the door.

Chapter Four

Gloria's heart pounded faster and harder than her feet as she flew down the path and across the lawn to the lodge, her sweater flung over her shoulders. How could she have been so forgetful about the time? She had meant to leave the cabin early and find Tim and tell him—if it wasn't too late already. What if his parents had told him that the Belvederes didn't *have* any nieces or female cousins? What if he already knew that she had lied to him? She dashed up the steps of the lodge and across the front porch. "Please, God," she prayed, gasping for breath, "let Tim be by himself, so that I can explain. Let his parents be late or off somewhere or . . ."

"Hi! Over here!"

Gloria turned. Tim was sitting on the deck overlooking the lake with a middle-aged man and woman who could only be his parents. Tim was grinning broadly as he waved, and Gloria's first reaction was one of relief. At least he didn't know *yet*. But the next instant, the relief turned to consternation. Now she would be doubly humiliated! She would have to confess her lie not only to Tim but to his parents, too —and they would probably tell the Belvederes! The thought of it made her want to turn and flee.

"Hey, come on, Gloria," Tim called again, insistently. "We've been waiting for you."

Feet dragging, Gloria walked slowly across the deck. Tim's mother had a nice smile, she thought dully. It was just like Tim's. And his father had that same look of poised self-assurance that she admired so much in Tim. Under other circumstances, she was sure that she would like the O'Neals very much.

"Gloria, I'd like you to meet my mother and father, Mr. and Mrs. O'Neal," Tim said formally, when Gloria reached the table. "Gloria is a . . . a kind of special friend," he added, with a tender look, reaching for her hand.

Gloria felt a soft warmth spreading inside her, quieting her fear a little. It *had* to be love that she heard in Tim's voice. And if he loved her, perhaps he could forgive her. "I . . . it's nice to meet you," she said shyly.

"It's nice to meet *you*, Gloria," Mrs. O'Neal said, taking Gloria's hand. "I know that Tim has been lonely, working here at the lodge this summer. You've helped to take the edge off that loneliness."

Mr. O'Neal smiled proudly. "I don't know when Tim has had time to be lonely, Elizabeth," he said to his wife. "Learning the ropes here at the lodge has taken a lot of his time, I'm sure." He turned to Gloria. "Tim didn't spend a lot of time playing around this summer, did he?"

"No, sir," Gloria said. "We only spent time together when he was finished working." She blushed. Suddenly it began to seem very warm on the deck, and she slipped out of her sweater. Under the table, Tim reached for her hand.

Mr. O'Neal nodded. "You know, when Tim decided last spring that he wanted to learn everything there was to know about the resort business—from the ground up—I wasn't sure he had the backbone to stick with it." He leaned back and looked appraisingly at Tim. "But I have to say, son, from all reports you've done a fine job. It isn't easy for a young man to step into the family business and make his co-workers accept him as if he were one of them, but you've managed to do it. I take my hat off to you."

Dumbfounded, Gloria stared at Tim. "'Step into the family business'?"

"Listen, Gloria, I'm sorry," Tim said, putting one arm on the back of Gloria's chair. "I know I should have told you, but I... Well, it just felt so good to know that you accepted and liked me for myself, without knowing that my family owned this place. So I put off telling you. It's been bothering me for weeks, but I couldn't seem to find a way to tell you."

"Your parents own Rainbow Lodge?" Gloria whispered. She felt as if the world had suddenly turned upside down.

"Tim, you really ought to have..." Tim's mother began.

"Not just Rainbow Lodge, young lady," Tim's father said, sitting up straighter, "but a whole string of resorts. All just as fine as this one."

"Is it okay?" Tim asked anxiously, in a low voice, touching her shoulder. Under the table, his hand tightened around hers. "I mean, you're not mad or anything, are you, Gloria? I figured that it wouldn't matter to you." He laughed a little. "It's going to be so good to relax and stop pretending... and know that we can accept each other exactly as we are. You have no idea how tough it's been the last few weeks, knowing that I was keeping something from you."

Gloria opened her mouth to say *But I'm keeping something from you, too. I'm not who you think I am.* But her throat closed around the words. She couldn't tell Tim the truth about herself—not now! If she did, he would surely believe that the whole thing was part of an elaborate setup to fool him, so that he wouldn't think she was after his money! What a horrible, complicated mess! Things just kept getting worse!

She looked across the table at the O'Neals, half-hoping that they would rescue her from her lie. "I understand that you know the Belvederes," she said in a small voice.

Mrs. O'Neal smiled. "Not really, dear. Mrs. Belvedere and I see each other socially from time to time, and we're both members of the Opera Guild. But we're not close friends. Please give your aunt my regards, and tell her that I hope to see her more often in the fall, when we move to Glenwood." She leaned forward, and Gloria could smell her expensive perfume. "And I do hope that you'll forgive my son for his innocent little masquerade. It wasn't very nice of him, but I'm glad that it has turned out well in the end."

"Yes, ma'am," Gloria said. She swallowed. She loved Tim, but would he still love her when he found out she wasn't related to the Belvederes, that her own family was nowhere near as wealthy?

Tim's fingers held hers tightly. "Forgiven?" he asked.

Gloria nodded. She could forgive Tim, but would he ever forgive her? Now she couldn't tell him the truth! She would just have to go on pretending.

"Gloria, this is absolutely crazy," Nancy was saying emphatically. "You've *got* to tell him! I mean, he's obviously going to find out sooner or later. He needs to hear it from you—right away."

Angie squirmed. She understood Nancy Colton's point of view, but couldn't Nancy and the others see that Gloria needed their support and help right now, not a lecture?

"I know you're right," Gloria moaned tearfully. She was sitting on Angie's bunk, and Angie had put her arm around her shoulders. "I keep trying to tell him, but somehow I just can't do it."

"Well, maybe you don't have to do it this weekend," Angie said.

Gloria looked up hopefully, wondering what Angie had in mind? "I don't?"

"Well, maybe not. I mean, of course you have to tell him eventually. But maybe it would be better if you waited until both of you got to Glenwood. By that time, you'll know each other a lot better, and it really won't matter to Tim who your family is." She smiled a little wistfully. "And anyway, this is a kind of magical weekend, isn't it? Maybe something really good will happen. Maybe your fairy godmother will come along and wave her magic wand over you, like Cinderella, and your troubles with Tim will be over."

Gloria stared at her, thinking of the hours of fairy-tale dreaming she'd been doing since she met Tim. "How did you know that I sometimes think of myself as Cinderella?" she whispered. "I realize it's a kind of a childish thing to do, but . . ."

Angie blushed and looked down. "Sometimes I daydream about myself that way, too. And I don't think it's childish at all. I mean, every one of us wants to be somebody special for somebody we care about. If you want to know the truth, I'd really like to be somebody special for Glenn St. Clair." She let out a tiny, embarrassed laugh. She'd never shared the way she felt about Glenn before, and she didn't know how the others were going to respond. "He's kind of . . . kind of like a prince, to me."

From the other end of the cabin, Rayne whistled. "Glenn St. Clair. Wow! You sure set your sights high, Angie Maroni. He *is* a *real* prince."

Angie sighed. Rayne was right. "I know," she said with resignation in her voice. "It's really kind of stupid to hope that anything might ever happen between us—especially after what happened today."

Gloria stared at her. "What happened today? Was it worse than what happened to me with Tim's parents?"

Angie shrugged, blushing, as she remembered. "I just knocked Glenn off his feet, that's all." She made a wry face. "And not with the sheer force of my personality, either." She told them about arriving at the parking lot in Tony's souped-up car, about climbing out the window and falling into Glenn's arms, and about Shannon Welles's advice to Glenn not to be seen with her.

"Yeah, well, everybody at Glenwood knows that Shannon Welles is a stuck-up snob," Nancy retorted. Angie looked at her in surprise. Was that true? She had thought that she only felt that way because she was jealous of Shannon.

"And not a very *nice* stuck-up snob, at that," Rayne added. "She's got a terrible reputation for loving and leaving. She must have broken a hundred hearts last year alone."

Angie almost smiled. It made her feel a whole lot better to discover that her bunkmates were on her side. "Well, from where I was sitting, it looked as if she was zeroing in on number one hundred and one," she said, remembering how Shannon's blond hair had brushed Glenn's cheek and the possessive way she had stroked his shoulder. "I can't help wishing that Glenn would see what's *really* inside her." *And what's inside me,* she thought, *under all this stuff about my reputation and my no-good family. I wish* my *fairy godmother would come along this weekend.*

She turned back to Gloria. "Anyway, all I wanted to say was that if you don't think you can tell Tim now, don't. And if I can help, I'd be glad to do whatever I can." She flashed Gloria a knowing, lopsided grin. "Tony once showed me how to hot-wire a car. How would you like me to wire up that white Porsche in the parking lot so that you can take *him* out?"

Gloria couldn't help giggling, feeling a strange tug at her heart. Angie Maroni, the girl from the wrong side of the tracks, the girl who always seemed tough as leather and hard as nails, seemed to understand what Gloria was going through better than her best friend, Nancy.

"Well, I don't think I need to drive that Porsche," Gloria joked, "but I really appreciate—"

She was suddenly interrupted by the sound of voices in front of the cabin.

"Well, I don't know how to answer," a puzzled male voice was saying. "I . . . I guess I haven't thought about it before. I mean, I guess I've just *done* it and haven't thought about *how* to do it. I mean . . ." The voice trailed off lamely.

"Maybe now's a good time to think about it. It's a pretty important activity, you know. When you stop to think about it, we couldn't run our lives without it. I mean, there probably wouldn't be any babies born without it, would there?" It was Lani Connors's voice.

With a horrified glance at one another, Gloria, Nancy, Rayne, and Angie got up and tiptoed to the door. They pressed their ears to it, listening.

"What in the world do you suppose she's *asked* him?" Nancy whispered. "You don't think she's asked about . . . about . . . Well, *you* know."

"I don't know," Gloria whispered back. "But he sounds pretty uncomfortable, doesn't he?"

"Well, sure, I guess it's sort of important," the boy said. He cleared his throat uneasily. ". . . Biologically speaking, that is. And I suppose I think about doing it sometimes. It's just that . . ."

"Oh, really?" Lani asked, in an arch tone. "How *often* do you think about doing it?"

Gloria opened the door a little wider and peered through. Lani was standing on her tiptoes, thrusting a microphone under the nose of Dave Carstairs. Gloria remembered Dave from U.S. history class last fall—only last fall he had been pudgy and pimply and shy. This summer he was tall and good-looking and very muscular in a pair of safari shorts and a short-cut T-shirt.

"Well, I . . . I suppose I think about it at least . . . at

least once a day, or something like that." Avoiding Lani's questioning gaze, Dave rubbed the toe of his tennis shoe in the dirt. He looked utterly miserable. What *had* Lani asked?

"Only once a day?" Lani's voice held an amused taunt. "You mean to say that you have girls around you at school all day, and you only think of it *once* a day?" She laughed skeptically. "Come on now, Dave, you look like a normal guy. Who are you trying to kid?"

Dave thrust his hands into the pockets of his shorts and looked even more miserable. "Well, uh . . . he whispered, "I . . ."

"Listen, Gloria," Nancy hissed into Gloria's ear, "we've *got* to stop this! There's no telling *what* she's asked him!"

Gloria nodded. "I'm with you," she said, stepping back.

Nancy opened the door and went out, with Gloria and the others close behind. "Well, hi!" she said brightly.

Dave looked up with a relieved, boy-am-I-glad-to-see-you expression. "Hi!" he said.

"What's going on?" Nancy asked casually. She stepped between Lani and Dave.

"Oh, nothing," Lani said, with a careless grin. She hooked the microphone onto her belt. "Just doing a little research, that's all."

Dave frowned. "Listen," he said to Nancy, lowering his voice, "if this girl is a friend of yours, I think you'd better find out what she's doing. Her questions are pretty embarrassing, if you want to know the truth."

Gloria stepped up behind Lani. "Lani, let's go in the cabin where you can tell us what you've been up to," she whispered urgently.

Lani pulled away. "I haven't been 'up to' anything," she retorted, in an irritated voice. "I've just been asking a few questions, that's all. It's part of that research project I was telling you about this afternoon."

Gloria grabbed Lani's arm and began to pull her toward the cabin. "I think we need to know more about this research project of yours," she said. "Why don't we all go talk about it inside and let Dave go on and do whatever he was about to do when you stopped him."

"I don't see why we have to go into the cabin to talk about it," Lani objected, digging in her heels. "There's nothing secret about it. I mean, in addition to helping me find the perfect boyfriend, this is perfectly legitimate psychological research. I might even submit it as an article to *The Glenwood Call*." She held up her hands, pretending to hold a newspaper. "Study Reveals Boys' Attitudes about Love."

Dave scowled. "Somehow I don't think that *The Call* is a very good place to print stuff like that. It just so happens that I'm on the staff, and . . ."

Nancy looked up at Dave, narrowing her eyes. "Well, it just so happens that *I'm* the new editor," she said. "I'm the one who says what gets printed and what doesn't." She hesitated. "Do you mind if I ask what the question was that was so embarrassing?"

Dave blushed and kicked a rock. "Well . . ."

"Come on," Nancy urged. "What was it? How are we supposed to handle this if we don't know what she was asking?"

"Well, okay," Dave said reluctantly. "She asked me to describe the perfect kiss."

Nancy's eyes grew round with relief. "Oh, thank heaven!" she breathed.

" 'Thank heaven'?" Dave asked. "I mean, it's a pretty embarrassing question."

"But it's not as embarrassing as the question *we* thought she was asking," Nancy said.

"You didn't think . . . ?" Dave said in a horrified whisper.

Nancy nodded.

Dave turned bright red.

"Only once a day?" Nancy asked, her shoulders shaking with suppressed laughter.

"I don't see what's so funny," Lani said, in an offended tone, shaking off Gloria's restraining hand. "I mean, what's the big deal? It's a reasonable question, isn't it? As a matter of fact, it turned out to be a very *revealing* question." She opened her notebook. "You'd be surprised at the interesting answers I've been getting."

Gloria and Angie and Rayne exchanged meaningful looks. "Now?" Gloria whispered.

"Now," Angie said, with a giggle.

"Now," Rayne nodded.

"Hey!" Lani said indignantly, as Gloria and Angie, laughing, grabbed her arms and began to drag her toward the cabin door that Rayne was holding open for them. "Hey, you guys, get your hands off me! I protest! I . . ."

Nancy looked at Dave, whose face had turned a deep shade of purple. "We apologize. She's kind of new at this sort of thing."

"Yeah," Dave said, watching thoughtfully as Gloria and Angie pulled Lani through the door. "She sure is." He laughed. "Well, good luck. See you tonight at the barbecue."

"Bye," Nancy said, watching him go.

"You guys didn't have to get involved," Lani said, pouting. "Things were going along just fine without you."

"Listen, if we hadn't come out when we did," Gloria reminded her, "you can be sure that Dave would've told all the other guys to stay away from you and your questions." She picked up Lani's research notebook and leafed through it.

"Let's hear about those questions," Nancy said.

"More to the point," Rayne said suggestively, "let's hear about the answers. Did you *really* ask boys to describe the perfect kiss?"

Lani took the notebook away from Gloria. "Yes, I did. I'm not ashamed to admit it. And they gave me some pretty informative answers, too. I'll bet you can't even guess what they said."

The girls looked at each other. "What kind of answers?" they all asked at once.

Lani opened the notebook, looking important. "Well, one guy said that he'd describe the perfect kiss as blonde, blue eyed, and about five foot six."

Nancy chuckled. "Hey, that's pretty funny."

"And this other guy said he'd describe it as hard to get."

Gloria and Angie began to giggle.

"And somebody else said he'd describe it as . . ." She paused, and the tip of her nose grew pink.

"Yes?" Rayne pressed.

Lani hesitated.

"As . . . ?" Nancy prompted.

"Well, actually, he gave me a demonstration." Lani sighed dramatically. "My first kiss, if you don't count the time that Milton Pringle won two games of chess in a row from me and got so carried away with excitement that he kissed me—on the cheek."

"How was it?" Gloria asked. "Was it a good kiss?"

"How am I supposed to know?" Lani asked impatiently. "How can you compare kisses if you've never been kissed before—except by Milton Pringle, in the heat of a passionate chess game? I mean, I've got to collect more data before I can give you a scientific answer to that question."

"You know, maybe this research project isn't such a bad idea, after all," Nancy remarked thoughtfully. "What did Dave Carstairs say when you asked him?"

Lani consulted her notebook. "He said that he didn't think there was such a thing as a perfect kiss. 'If you love someone, and that person loves you back, then however you kiss each other, it'll be perfect.' That's what he said."

Gloria glanced at Nancy. Nancy was smiling a little, a kind of half-tender, half-wistful smile. But when she looked up and caught Gloria watching her, the smile disappeared. "Some answer," Nancy said sarcastically. "Sounds like he's been taking Mrs. Wiseman's psychology class."

"I think it's a perceptive answer," Angie said, wondering how Glenn would have answered the question. "I think it's the *only* answer. I'd like to know more about a guy who could come up with an answer like that."

"Well, maybe it is," Nancy retorted, coloring, "... perceptive, I mean. But I'll bet you'd find out that Dave Carstairs isn't any different than any other boy, once you got to know him. In the end, they all break somebody's heart."

"Are you sure that boys have a monopoly on heartbreaking?" Angie asked, thinking of Shannon Welles.

Nancy was quiet for a minute, looking at Angie. "Well, maybe not," she admitted.

"Listen, *I'm* sure of something," Rayne said, looking at her watch. "I'm sure that if we don't hurry, we're going to be late to the barbecue. And I'm anxious to see if Ginger Goodman really deserves all those nice things that people say about her." She pulled on a sweat shirt over her blouse and began to brush her hair. "Are you guys coming?"

"As soon as I find my sweater," Gloria said, searching the pile of clothes on her bunk. "Has anybody seen my red sweater? I could've sworn I packed it." She got down on her hands and knees and looked under the lower bunk. "Now, where do you suppose it is?" she said in a puzzled tone, still on her knees.

She looked up at Nancy, who was peering into a small mirror, putting on makeup. "Have you seen it, Nancy?"

Nancy shook her head. "Nobody else has been in the cabin but us," she said. "It's got to be here somewhere."

Angie could feel her face growing hot. It always happened this way. As soon as something was missing, she was under suspicion. "Do you want to look under my bunk?" Angie asked sulkily. "Or under my blankets, maybe?" She held her arms in the air with a brittle laugh. "Or maybe you'd even like to frisk me!"

Gloria stared at her. "Why should I want to frisk you?"

"To prove to yourself that I'm not a thief," Angie said defensively. "That's why."

"I don't need proof that you're not a thief," Gloria said. "I *know* you're not a thief." She looked soberly at Angie. "And I know something else, too," she added.

"What's that?" Angie asked, dropping her arms. She was close to tears.

"For such a tough kid, you've got very thin skin," Gloria said, slipping an arm around Angie's waist. "But, that's okay. We've got all weekend to toughen you up!"

"Hey, Gloria, did you put on your sweater when you went up to the lodge to meet Tim's parents?" Rayne asked. "Did you bring it back with you?"

Gloria hit her forehead with the heel of her hand. "Nope. That must be where it is," she exclaimed. "I left it on the back of my chair. I can't believe how careless I am!"

Angie felt a sudden sense of relief. She was glad that Gloria didn't think she was a thief, but it was even better that there was *proof* that she wasn't.

Chapter Five

Angie followed Gloria up the path to the Wigwam, where the barbecue was being held that night. The Wigwam was a huge canvas teepee painted with bright Indian markings and set up on a wooded hill not far from the lodge. It had been one of her favorite spots all summer, Gloria told Angie, because it overlooked the lake, and she and Tim had gone there sometimes to watch the sun set.

Tonight the falling sun was staining the water with beautiful colors of soft orange and mulberry, and Angie and Gloria stood for a few minutes, watching the colors fade to a softly muted gray-blue. Angie thought the lake and the mountains to the west were the most beautiful sight she had ever seen. The Maronis didn't take many vacations, and Rainbow

Lake was the farthest Angie had ever been away from home, except when she had gone to Los Angeles to stay with her sister's little boy when her sister went to the hospital to have another baby. Of course, Angie had been to the big park that straddled the mountain just above Glenwood, but never to a place like this, and the sight of the lake made her feel extraordinarily calm and peaceful.

The large, grassy clearing around the Wigwam was crowded with noisy kids and tables loaded with trays heaped full of Ginger's barbecued ribs and Texas-style beans. A huge bonfire was roaring in the middle of the clearing, the flames dancing high. Kids were lining up for food and looking around for places to sit on the ground.

Gloria took Angie with her to look for Ginger. They found her with her sleeves rolled up, supervising the tables.

"Can we help?" Gloria asked, after she had introduced Angie and Ginger.

"Oh, I don't think so," Ginger said, eyeing the tables critically. "We've got plenty of help." She gestured toward an empty tray, and a girl hurried to fill it up with fat, juicy sausages. "I'd say we're in pretty good shape, considering."

"Considering?"

"...Considering that Craig's ribs were slow getting done, I put too much salt in the beans, and we lost two big bowls of potato salad." Ginger ran her fingers distractedly through her reddish-brown hair. "But we've coped with so many disasters in this business that I guess I wouldn't know what to do if things went smoothly."

"How could you *lose* two bowls of potato salad?" Angie asked curiously. She admired Ginger. If those things had happened to her, she would have fallen apart.

"Beats me," Ginger said, shrugging. "Maybe we didn't lose them. Maybe we just didn't count right. Who knows?" She gestured toward the tables with a smile. "Anyway, there it is, folks—Goodman and Company's best culinary effort. Go for it." She smiled at Angie. "Nice to meet you, Angie. Have a good time tonight. And welcome to the senior class."

"Thank you," Angie said shyly. *Welcome to the senior class.* She smiled to herself. She was finally beginning to feel comfortable here as just one senior among many. Nobody was shunning her because of her family's history, and for the first time in her life she felt special and liked just for being herself.

Angie followed Ginger as they made their way across the clearing to line up at a table loaded with food. At the end of the line, they ran into a good-looking boy with a T-shirt that said RAINBOW LODGE across the front. Angie noticed Gloria's face light up when she saw him.

"Hi, Tim!" Gloria said happily. "This is one of my cabin mates, Angie. Angie, this is Tim O'Neal."

Angie and Tim said hello as they took their places in line. Tim was looking at Gloria with a tender expression that made Angie feel wistful. Wouldn't it be wonderful if someday Glenn looked at *her* that way? It didn't seem like a very realistic hope, but Angie wasn't about to let her thoughts dampen her spirits.

"Boy, did you make a big hit with my mother and father," Tim was saying to Gloria, as he slipped his arm around her waist. "They really liked you. They kept talking about how nice it was that you and I have so much in common."

"In common?" Gloria asked. Angie thought that she looked uneasy.

Tim laughed a little. "Oh, you know. Sometimes they make too big a deal about this high-society stuff. But they don't really mean anything by it. I guess it's all just a part of life in the fast lane." He laughed again, confidently. "But then, you already know about that."

A flush had risen on Gloria's face, and Angie, standing close to her as they helped themselves to potato salad, could sense Gloria's tension.

"Well, I'm glad they liked me," Gloria said, in a

strangled voice. She didn't look up. "I liked them, too. I just wish I were..." She swallowed hard, and for a second Angie thought she was going to blurt out the truth.

But she didn't. "I...I mean, I just wish I could have stayed longer," she stammered lamely.

"Well, there'll be another chance before long," Tim said, spearing a rack of ribs onto his paper plate and spooning barbecue sauce over it. "As a matter of fact, my mother mentioned the possibility of inviting the Belvederes over for dinner once we get settled in our new house. You're invited, too, and of course your parents. They'd like to meet some new people in the Glenwood area. What do you think of the idea?"

Gloria looked as if she considered it a *terrible* idea. "Well, maybe," Gloria said. She put a small spoonful of potato salad next to a tiny puddle of beans. She was quickly losing her appetite. "I...I'm not sure about my parents."

"How come?" Tim asked curiously. He added a pickle to his plate. "Don't you think they'd want to?"

"Well, I'm not sure," Gloria said, casting an anguished look at Angie. "I...I mean, they might be out of the country or..."

"Oo-o-ps!" Angie said. Suddenly, as if it had a mind of its own, her heavy paper plate slipped out of her hand. It landed, upside down, squarely on Tim's foot. A big gob of potato salad stuck to the toe of his sneaker, and a streak of muddy red bean juice stained his sock. He stared down at it.

"Oh, I'm sorry, Tim," Angie said, getting down on her hands and knees to clean up the mess. "I'm so incredibly clumsy sometimes." She scrubbed at his tennis shoe with a paper napkin. "I hope this isn't going to stain."

"Listen, Angie, don't worry about it," Tim said. "Come on, get up. It's okay. These sneakers have seen worse than a little potato salad." He bent over and picked up Angie's empty plate, then found her ribs halfway under the table. "Looks like you're going to have to start over again."

"Here, let me help," Gloria said quickly, with a profoundly grateful look at Angie. "I'll fix you another plate."

"Oh, I can do it," Angie said. "Really. It was all my fault, anyway."

"I *want* to," Gloria said fervently, heaping ribs and potato salad onto another plate. "After all, what are friends for?"

After they had eaten, all the seniors gathered in a big circle around the bonfire. It was completely dark now, and the leaping flames cast a soft orange glow over their faces. Gloria looked at Tim, lying on the grass beside her, his face happy and relaxed. If only she had the courage to tell him the truth right now, before another minute went by. Surely he would understand how it had happened.

She sighed. But what if Tim *didn't* understand? What if he thought she had been trying to trick him all along? She knew she had to tell him sooner or later. But maybe Angie was right. Maybe it would be better to wait until school had started. By that time she and Tim would know each other better, they would feel more comfortable together, and it wouldn't be such a big deal.

"Okay, everybody," Ms. Richards stood up and motioned for silence. She didn't look at all like a stern biology teacher tonight, in jeans and a plaid flannel shirt, her soft hair tumbling over her shoulder. Mr. Dawson was sitting on the ground nearby, smoking his pipe and watching her thoughtfully. "We're about to begin the seniors welcome ceremony," she said. "The supervisors are handing out candles to everyone. The idea is to light the candle of someone you *don't* know, as well as the candle of a friend. After all, one of the reasons we have this camp-out is to meet people we otherwise might not get to know."

"Come on, give us a break," one of the boys said disgustedly. "How come we have to do all this hokey stuff?"

"You don't *have* to do it," Ms. Richards said quietly. "But sometimes the most meaningful parts of our lives are the times we let ourselves indulge in a few sentimental rituals." Her grin took some of the seriousness out of her words. "Like hokey Thanksgiving and Christmas."

"Anyway, a little hokiness once in a while never hurt anybody," somebody else said. "Bring on the candles!" Some of the kids clapped.

After everyone had candles, they all stood up. A dozen people lit their candles at the bonfire and then went to their friends, to light *their* candles. Nancy came over to light Gloria's candle. "Here's to a wonderful senior year," she said. "And here's to a wonderful friend."

Gloria hugged her. There was a choking feeling in her throat. "Last year was really terrific," she said, thinking about all their good times as juniors. "But I know that this year will be even better."

After Nancy had gone, Gloria turned to Tim. "Here's to a wonderful senior year, Tim," she repeated softly, touching her flame to his candle.

"Thanks," he said, in a quiet voice, bending forward to kiss her on the cheek. "Did anyone ever tell you how pretty you are?"

Gloria felt like crying.

For a minute, Angie stood all alone with her candle in her hand, kids swirling around her excitedly, lighting each other's candles and exchanging good wishes for the year. Beside her, Gloria and Tim were engrossed in conversation, oblivious of everything else, and on the other side of the bonfire she could see Dave Carstairs lighting Nancy's candle and Rayne standing close to a boy who had his arm around her shoulders. The feeling of being special faded suddenly, leaving her cold and shivery in the darkness. Everybody here was part of somebody else—everybody but her. She felt very alone and more than a little foolish, standing there with her unlit candle among all the couples who were sharing such an important beginning.

"Hey, your candle isn't lit yet." A deep voice startled her. It was Glenn St. Clair. "How can you start the senior year when your candle isn't burning?"

Angie wanted to say, "Would you please light my candle," but the words wouldn't come.

"Well, are you waiting for lightning to strike?" Glenn asked, amusement in his voice. "Or will I do just as well?"

Angie held up her candle. It trembled and she tried to steady her hand. "Please," she said. It was all she could manage.

Glenn bent toward her. "Here's to a wonderful senior year," he said softly, touching the tip of his lighted candle to hers. The flame flickered and almost went out, but it held, gleaming brightly in the dark.

"Thank you," Angie whispered. "I...I wish the same to you." Her mouth felt as if it were full of dry sand, and her heart was pounding.

"How could senior year be anything but wonderful?" Glenn asked, his eyes on hers.

"You're right. It will be," Angie responded. She couldn't think of anything else to say. The magic of the firelight enveloped them in a soft glow, and she stood there looking into Glenn's eyes, mesmerized, their candles flickering in the dark between them.

Suddenly they were interrupted. "Well, *there* you are, Glenn. I've been looking all over for you." Shannon Welles sounded impatient. "Pete and Sarah are waiting for us down by the lake. Really, this ceremonial stuff is too boring—we're all going swimming off the rocks." Her laugh tinkled merrily as she reached for Glenn's hand. "It'll be our own private party."

Angie shivered and with an effort pulled her eyes away from Glenn's. Beside her, Gloria suddenly leaned toward Shannon. "Swimming off the rocks?" she asked. "In the dark? Isn't that a little dangerous?"

"Well, what of it?" Shannon asked coldly, adding with a wicked smile, "Life's most exciting when you live dangerously, don't you think?" She laughed and gave his arm a gentle tug. "Come on, Glenn."

Angie knew what Shannon was hinting at, and a hard little knot of anger worked its way up her throat. Then her anger dissolved into jealousy as she thought of Shannon and Glenn swimming together in the dark water, touching each other, laughing together. At that instant her candle flame flickered and went out.

Glenn looked at Shannon. "I'm not sure I want to go swimming right now," he said quietly. "Paul Mitchell brought his guitar, and he's going to play in a little while."

Shannon snorted. "Really, Glenn. I *said* that all this campfire stuff was boring, and I meant it." She came closer, and Angie could hear the promise in her voice. "There are so many more *exciting* things that we could be doing." She ran her finger back and forth along Glenn's bare arm.

Glenn frowned, unable to decide what to do. "Well, I guess I ought to come along to keep you out of trouble," he said at last.

"I don't care *why* you come, as long as you come," Shannon said. And the two of them disappeared into the darkness.

"That is definitely *not* cool," Tim said. "It's dangerous to swim off the rocks."

"Well, Glenn's got a pretty good head," Gloria said. "I don't think he'll let them get into real trouble." She looked searchingly at Angie. "Hey, Angie, are you okay?"

Angie looked down at her candle. "Would you mind lighting my candle again?" she asked quietly, trying not to sound as hurt as she felt. "It went out."

After the candle-lighting ceremony, they sat down around the fire again. Paul Mitchell, the boy who had stood with his arm around Rayne, got out his guitar and others brought out a banjo and a dulcimer. Angie sat cross-legged on the grass, letting her husky contralto blend in softly with the other voices to the traditional folk tunes. Sparks from the fire danced high into the air, like fireworks on the Fourth of July, and the faces around her were happy ones. But she still felt lonely and separate, thinking of Glenn and Shannon, swimming together.

"Mind if I sit down?" Stephanie asked during a lull between songs. Without waiting for an answer, she sank down on the grass beside Angie. "Having fun?"

Angie nodded. In spite of her loneliness, it *was* fun. "I've never really been out of the city before," she said.

"Well, tomorrow ought to be quite a day for all you city kids," Stephanie said, folding her feet under her.

"It ought to be really different."

"What's happening tomorrow?" Angie asked curiously.

"Tomorrow," Stephanie said, "we're going for a hike."

"Hey, that's great," Angie said. "You're right. It will be different for me." She had the feeling that most of the kids had been on hikes before, at summer camp or on vacations with their parents in the mountains or the desert. But she'd never gone to summer camp, and the only vacation her family had ever taken was the weekend they'd gone to Santa Cruz and stayed in that dumpy motel by the boardwalk. That was before Dad got sentenced to Lompoc. Angie's throat tightened. She didn't want to think about *that* now, on top of everything else.

Lani Connors came up and sat down with them, dumping her shoulder bag onto the grass. "Hey, did I hear somebody mention a hike?"

"Yeah. Around the lake," Stephanie said.

Lani looked alarmed. "Around *that* lake?" she asked, pointing out into the darkness. "That's a *big* lake!"

Stephanie nodded. "Right. It's a long hike. We start at the lodge after breakfast and take our lunches with us. We ought to be back about three, in plenty of time for some volleyball or tennis in the afternoon—if you're not all worn out. Make sure you wear comfortable shoes, hiking boots or a pair of good jogging shoes." She leaned forward, looking curiously at Lani. "Say, aren't you Marcia Connors's sister? I think you're in one of my cabins."

"Right," Lani said, with a matter-of-fact nod. "I'm the plain one in the family."

Stephanie looked puzzled. "You don't look so plain to me."

"It's the firelight," Lani explained. "It makes everybody look pretty. Even me." She held up her hand. "Really. Scientific fact."

Listening, Angie laughed. She admired Lani's realistic way of looking at things. If *she* could be half as realistic, she probably wouldn't be disappointed so often—the way she had been tonight when Glenn went off with Shannon. She had *known* that it was silly to hope that he might want to stay at the campfire with her, but it still disappointed her that he hadn't. "Speaking of science, how's your research project going?" she asked Lani. "Got any more good answers?"

"Research project?" Stephanie asked with a curious look. "What kind of research project?"

"Listen, not only have I got some more good answers," Lani said earnestly, "but I've thought of a couple of even more terrific questions."

"Lani is trying to figure out all the characteristics of the perfect boyfriend," Angie told Stephanie. "She's got this list of questions, and she's asking all the boys to answer them."

Stephanie peered at Lani in the firelight. "Are you sure that's such a good idea?" she asked dubiously. "I mean, it seems so *obvious*. It looks like you're so hard up for a boyfriend that you can't figure out any other way."

Lani shrugged. "Well, of course it's obvious," she said. "But when you're Marcia Connors's plain little sister, you *have* to be obvious. If you're not obvious, you're ignored. And anyway, how are you supposed to find the best *possible* boyfriend if you don't make sure that people know you're available?"

"Good point," Stephanie said thoughtfully. She scrambled to her feet. "Well, listen, you guys, I'm going to go down and check on my cabins. I'm sorry I didn't get to yours this afternoon, but I'll stop by before lights-out tonight. See you later."

Lani stood up and stretched. "Are you ready to go to the cabin, Angie? If you are, let's walk together. I'm pooped."

Angie stood up and smiled. "Sure, I'm pretty tired, too. It's been a long day." And what a day it had been. It seemed like ages ago when Tony had dropped her off in the school parking lot, ages ago when she fell right into Glenn St. Clair's arms. All in all, this was turning out to be an exciting weekend, and she had three more days to look forward to.

Chapter Six

"Hey, wake up! It's time to get up."

"Oh, God, it can't be. What time is it?"

"Was that the breakfast bell? I can't believe that it was the breakfast bell."

"How could it be time for breakfast? The birds aren't even awake yet!"

"What do you mean, the birds aren't awake yet? Didn't you hear that stupid woodpecker? He's been doing surgery on that pine tree just outside the window ever since dawn."

Angie rolled over on her cot and pulled the pillow over her head, wishing that the voices would stop and let her sleep. And then she remembered where she was and jumped out of bed. The sun was streaming in through the screen, and the morning air felt cool and delicious. This was Rainbow Lake, these were her new friends, and today they were going for a hike.

"Hey, isn't it an absolutely terrific day?" Gloria asked from her top bunk, stretching. Her frizzy blond hair stood up all over her head.

"I don't know," Lani groaned, putting her head back under the blanket. "It's too early to tell." She poked one eye out. "If you really want to know, ask that stupid woodpecker. He's been up long enough to know."

Stephanie knocked at the door and stuck her head in. "Everybody up!" she ordered cheerfully. "Breakfast at the lodge in half an hour. Don't forget what today is. We want to get an early start."

Rayne looked puzzled. "An early start? What's happening today?" Angie glanced at Rayne. Even with no makeup and her hair all tousled, she looked beautiful.

"Time for action!" Lani said. She jumped up and stood at attention in the middle of the floor in her rumpled pajamas, puffing out her cheeks and blowing a pretend bugle. "*Ta ta ta ta-ta-ta.*" She raised her arm in a grand gesture. "Get your tickets for the super safari right here, folks! The elephants are departing from the back door of the lodge right after breakfast. If you miss the elephants, you have to walk." She turned and began to parade back and forth in front of the bunks, waving an imaginary banner. "Everybody up and fall in for the great Rainbow Lake hiking party!"

There was a loud chorus of groans. "Hike!" Nancy said, in a tone of mock horror, covering her eyes. "You mean, we actually have to *walk* someplace today?"

"Exactly eight-point-four miles," Stephanie reported. "Mr. Dawson says that he's clocked it with his pedometer." She started out the door. "See you at breakfast," she said over her shoulder. The door slammed behind her.

There was a stunned silence. "Eight-point-four miles?" Rayne said, in a hushed voice. "Give us a break—that's nearly *ten* miles. We have to walk ten miles today?"

Gloria tumbled out of her bunk, wondering if Tim was going to be waiting on tables this morning at breakfast. "It's not even *close* to ten miles, Rayne," she said, pulling on her jeans energetically. "It's only a little over eight miles." She grinned. "See? It's all in how you look at it."

"I've decided that I don't *want* to look at it," Rayne said emphatically, sliding down in her bed. "I have every intention of staying here and looking at the lake from the beach, thank you. Oo-h-h!" she screeched, as Gloria yanked off her blankets. Angie, pulling her sweat shirt over her head, heard the sounds of a brief scuffle and loud giggling, then the thump of a body on the floor. She turned around in time to see Gloria and Rayne play-fighting on the floor.

"Okay, okay," Rayne said, gasping for breath, as Gloria threatened to tickle her again. "I give up. I give up. I'll go. Just give me a minute to get used to the idea."

Angie sat down on the edge of her bunk, trying to decide whether she should wear the sandals she had worn yesterday or the ragged old tennis shoes she had thrown into her duffel bag as an afterthought. The sandals wouldn't be very good for hiking, but the tennis shoes were really worn out. It was a tough choice.

After a minute, Gloria came over and sat down beside her, a little out of breath from her tussle with Rayne. "Ready for breakfast?" she asked.

"As soon as I figure out what to put on my feet," Angie said. She gave an embarrassed laugh. "I guess it's a matter of choosing between my vanity or my comfort." She stuck her feet into her worn tennis shoes and looked at them. Her little toe poked through a hole in the side. Hastily, she kicked them off, thinking of Glenn. "I think I'll just wear my sandals," she said. She sighed. Shannon Welles would probably have the latest in jogging shoes, not to mention a color-coordinated hiking outfit.

"Hey, I've got just the thing," Gloria said suddenly, jumping up. "A new pair of running shoes." She ran over to her bunk and pulled them out from under the bed. "Here. Try them on," she said, thrusting the shoes at Angie. "Your feet look about the same size as mine."

"Oh, no, Gloria. I can't wear your shoes," Angie protested. "Especially not such *nice* ones."

"Sure you can wear them," Gloria said matter-of-factly. "See? It's easy. All you have to do is put them on, lace them up, and *voilà!* You're wearing my shoes!"

Angie shook her head. "That isn't what I mean," she said, in a low voice. "I mean, I can't borrow these. What would you wear?"

Gloria stuck her feet out. She was wearing another, slightly worn, pair of jogging shoes. "I'm all set," she said carelessly. "In fact, these will be more comfortable. They're already broken in." She put her arm around Angie's shoulders. "Never look a gift horse in the hoof," she added. "And anyway, after what you did last night..."

Angie blushed. "Really, Gloria, I didn't do it on purpose. It was an accident." She laughed, remembering how silly Tim's shoe had looked, topped with a mushy glob of potato salad and streaked with bean juice.

"Well, accidental or planned, it was a lifesaver," Gloria declared. She shook her head soberly. "You know, sometimes I think that I'm in this thing so deeply, I'll never get out. Last night I was about to make it worse by telling some stupid lie about my folks going to Europe or something." She shuddered. "My father's a mailman, and my mother's a nurse, for heaven's sake. I mean, they're really terrific people, but the only way they'd ever get to Europe would be to win first prize in a contest." She took a deep breath and smiled crookedly. "Anyway, Angie, thanks again. I'm sorry you had to drop your potato salad on Tim's foot to keep me from telling another lie, but I'm really glad you did. You saved me from myself."

Angie blushed. "Anytime," she said.

Gloria looked at her. "I have a suggestion for you, if you don't mind."

"Suggest away."

"Well, I was just going to suggest that you . . . uh, that you change your lipstick. That orange shade you've been wearing is just a little . . . well, overpowering." Gloria stood up. "I've got this great new pink that I think would look perfect on you. Want to try it?"

Angie stared at her. "I . . . I guess so," she said. When she did, she had to admit that Gloria was right. The pink looked so much softer than the orange. Though a little embarrassed that she hadn't realized it herself, she was grateful for Gloria's concern.

"Ta ta ta ta-ta-ta!" Lani trumpeted again, from the door. "All ashore that's going ashore! Breakfast line forms to the left. Everybody march!"

Tim *was* waiting tables in the dining room, Gloria discovered. Her heart skipped a beat as she watched him pour a glass of tomato juice for her. Then she sat down at a table with Stephanie, Ginger, and Elaine Gregory. She knew Elaine slightly from Drama Club last year. Ms. Richards had introduced her yesterday as one of the bunk supervisors.

"Hi," Tim said, leaning over the back of Gloria's chair. "The usual?"

"Hi," Gloria said shyly, remembering how he had kissed her last night at the door to the cabin, after they had come back from the Wigwam. "Yes, please." She looked at him. "Are you going on the hike this morning?"

Tim nodded, with a grin. "The manager says it's okay for me to take the rest of the day off. How about that?"

"That's wonderful!" Gloria said. Then she sobered. Maybe she *shouldn't* wait until school started, after all. Maybe today, on the hike, would be a good time to tell him.

"I'll meet you outside after breakfast," Tim said, putting a stack of pancakes on Gloria's plate and pouring maple syrup over them. Gloria sometimes brought the twins over to the lodge for breakfast, and Tim had always waited on them. He knew what Gloria liked.

"Hey, that's what I call service," Stephanie said enviously. She glanced at Tim's retreating back as he walked across the room. "He's kind of cute."

Gloria sighed. "I know," she said, watching him wistfully.

"Hey, talking about cute," Elaine Gregory said from across the table, "you should have seen the male lead in the movie my boyfriend, Zack, made this summer." She whistled. "He was *really* cute. He looked like a genuine cowboy—and sometimes he acted like one, too. All the girls in the cast went crazy over him."

"What movie?" Gloria asked, puzzled.

"Well, Zack and I went to Arizona for a couple of months this summer," Elaine explained. She reached for the milk and poured it over her cereal. Her dark brown hair was pulled back into a ponytail, and she had a deep tan. Gloria thought that whatever she had done this summer, it had certainly made her look older and more self-confident. "Zack was shooting a low-budget western in a ghost town in the middle of the desert," Elaine went on, "and we spent a lot of time riding through canyons, looking for shooting locations and stuff like that." She laughed. "I'm still pulling cactus thorns out of my arms."

Ginger ran her fingers through her reddish-brown hair. "Wow, that sounds like fun," she said. "Except for the cactus, of course. What a terrific way to start your college career. The rest of us ordinary working mortals really envy you."

"Where are you going to college, Elaine?" Gloria askcd. Elaine had a reputation for taking her studies very seriously.

"Elaine's been accepted at Stanford," Stephanie explained proudly, reaching for the butter. "But she's going to be around Glenwood a lot this year. In fact, she's agreed to tutor me."

Elaine gave Stephanie a playful shove. "Tutor you? I thought I just agreed to *tutor*, period. I didn't know that you were going to be my one-and-only client. That wasn't part of the bargain."

"Listen," Stephanie said earnestly, "if getting an A average the second time around is the only way I can get admitted to Northwestern next year, I intend to spend every spare minute *this* year with a book in my hand." There was a disbelieving hoot from Ginger, and Stephanie turned on her. "You think I'm kidding?" she said. "Listen, I miss Alex so much that I would do *anything* to get into Northwestern." She looked forlorn. "Even do senior year over again. Even have Elaine tutor me." She shuddered. "Even study."

"I'll believe it when I see it," Ginger said skeptically. She reached over and stole a bite of croissant from Stephanie's plate and chewed it with thoughtful concentration. "Nope, not *nearly* as good as my croissants," she concluded. "Not quite as flaky."

"How *are* your croissants?" Elaine asked. "The last I heard, you were going to open a bakery this summer."

Ginger nodded. "I did, and they're fine, thank you."

Gloria agreed. "Ginger brought some croissants to a planning meeting the other day. They were pretty good."

"Actually," Ginger corrected Gloria, arching her eyebrows, "they were *very* good. The bakery is doing extremely well, and once we get our advertising campaign under way, I expect it to do even better. And the gourmet catering business is coming along, too. I've already got contracts for three dinners next month. I'm pretty pleased with the way things are going." She turned to Elaine. "What did you think about the food last night?"

Elaine wrinkled her nose. "Well, the beans were a little salty," she said, "and the potato salad ran out just as I got there." She waved her hand. "So-so, I guess."

"Oh, come on!" Ginger looked offended. "Wasn't it any better than that?"

Elaine laughed. "It was wonderful, Ginger," she said. "I was just kidding."

"Well, that's all right then," Ginger said, pushing her plate away. "Hey, you guys, I keep forgetting to tell you I got a letter from Kit and Lori last week, and they said to tell you both hello."

Stephanie looked up. "Really? Where are they?"

"They're in New York for vacation before they start college," Ginger said. "I put them on the plane a month ago, with a big suitcase full of ginger cookies."

Just then, Ms. Richards and Mr. Dawson came up to the table. "If you girls are ready," Ms. Richards said, glancing at her watch, "I think we'd better get this hike started. Mr. Dawson says that the forecast calls for thundershowers later this afternoon, and it might be a good idea if we start a little earlier than we planned."

Stephanie pushed back her chair with a sigh. "Okay, Gloria," she said resignedly. "It's safari time. Tell Lani to rustle up her elephants."

Angie hurried to catch up with Rayne Ramirez. They had been hiking for about fifteen minutes now, and Rayne, on the path ahead of Angie, was walking with shoulders slumped and head bowed, hardly looking to either side. When Rayne had gotten up early in the morning she had seemed full of good spirits, but now, Angie thought, she seemed very subdued. Angie wondered if anything had happened at breakfast. "Mind if I walk with you for a while?" she asked.

Rayne shook her head. "I'm not sure that I'm very good company," she said, "but you're welcome, if you want to."

They walked along together in silence. Off to the left, Angie could see the lake glinting through the pine trees, bright in the morning sun. To her right, the ground rose up steeply as the path cut its way along the foot of a hill. The pines smelled sweet and fresh, and Angie took a deep breath, relishing the spicy fragrance.

Beside her, Rayne stumbled, and Angie caught her arm. "You okay?" she asked.

Rayne shook her head, and Angie could see the tears in her eyes. "No, I'm not okay," she admitted.

"Want to tell me about it?" Angie felt a little awkward asking. Except for her friend Coralee, she hadn't ever confided in anybody. She always figured that if somebody told her personal stuff, she'd have to tell them personal stuff, and she couldn't really talk about herself without talking about her family. And talking about her family, especially about her brother and her father, was hard. But this weekend was making her feel more open, and right now she really wanted to know what was bothering Rayne. "Maybe it'll help to talk about it," she added.

"It's kind of a long story," Rayne said.

"You've got eight-point-four miles to tell it in," Angie reminded her with a grin. They came to a sharp turn in the path, and a breathtaking view of the lake opened out in front of them. They stood for a minute, looking out over the water.

Then Rayne said, "Do you remember what I said yesterday about boys not understanding what friends are all about?"

"Yes," Angie said. "You said that they didn't know what it meant to stand by somebody." *I remembered it because it was important to me,* she added silently to herself. *It would be wonderful to have somebody stand by* me.

"Well, I had somebody in mind," Rayne said sadly. "His name is Paul. Paul Mitchell."

"The good-looking guy you were with last night, the one who played the guitar?"

"Right. Paul and I have been going together for about a year now, and until this summer, things were really good between us. He's the sort of guy who always wants me to be my best, if you know what I mean. He demands a lot of himself, and he demands a lot of me. And since I push myself hard, too, we've always seemed like a really good match."

Angie nodded, but she wasn't sure she understood. Nobody in her life had ever really demanded that she do her best. In fact, it was sort of the other way around. Do just enough to get by was what everybody said. Don't put out any special effort. Don't push yourself.

"Anyway, that was how it was between Paul and me—until my friend Monica got pregnant," Rayne said.

"Monica Woollery?" Angie was surprised. She remembered Monica from home ec. class. Monica had dropped out of school last year after she got pregnant. Angie had felt sorry for her, even though she hadn't known her that well.

Rayne nodded. "Monica wasn't my best friend back then, but I knew her. She was in my gym class.

When she found out she was pregnant, I was the only one she could talk to. So we got sort of close, and she began to tell me what was happening to her."

A couple of girls caught up with them and paused for a minute to look at the lake. Then they went on, giggling noisily. Angie and Rayne started to walk again. Angie remembered what had happened to Monica. By the time school was out for the year, everyone was gossiping about her being pregnant.

Rayne went on with her story. "Monica decided right away that the guy wouldn't make a good father, but her folks are still giving her a hard time, pressuring her to get married."

Off the trail a short distance, Angie could hear the musical splash of a waterfall among the rocks. It made her feel sad to think of Monica having her baby all alone, with no husband. Angie's sister had gotten pregnant when Angie was just a kid, but she still remembered it. There was a big family fight, and then a big wedding. Her sister had cried all through the ceremony.

"Is she going to do it?" Angie asked finally. "Get married, I mean."

Rayne shook her head. "She's trying to go it alone. I really admire Monica's courage. She's living with her brother and working and going to natural childbirth classes." She smiled. "I'm going with her, as a matter of fact. Since the baby's father isn't around, I'm her birth coach. And she's making plans to have the baby adopted after it's born. She says she knows that she can't give the baby the kind of family it deserves, so the best thing to do is to give it to a family who really wants a child. I think she's brave."

Angie picked up a fallen branch, frosted with gray-green lichens. Monica *was* brave, Angie thought. "Yeah, I agree," she said, thinking about her sister. "It takes a lot of backbone to stand up to that kind of pressure from your family." She frowned. "But I still don't see how any of this is connected to you and Paul."

Rayne swiveled around to face her. "It's Paul's attitude toward Monica."

"His attitude?"

"You see, he's got this stupid idea that Monica's bad reputation is going to rub off on me. Ever since we became close friends, he's told me that I shouldn't get so involved with her."

Angie took a deep breath. "Oh," she said. "I see."

"I just wish Paul could see how important this is to me," Rayne burst out angrily. "I like Monica, and I admire her. And this is a good experience for me. I want to be a doctor some day, and being with Monica as she goes through this is teaching me a lot. But Paul just can't seem to get it through his head that friends stand by each other. This morning at breakfast we had another huge argument about it, and he really got mad. He thinks that people will begin to judge me by Monica's reputation. And this morning he said that I was going to have to choose between him and Monica. He said I couldn't have both."

Angie swallowed. It seemed as though *everything* was a matter of reputation. There wasn't any way you could get away from it. "Does he *know* Monica?" she asked.

"Well, no," Rayne admitted. "I mean, he's met her, but he doesn't know her the way I do."

Angie picked up a small, smooth rock and turned it over in her hand. On the underside was the imprint of a fossilized shell, set deeply and cleanly into the stone. A long time ago, a creature had left its mark on the rock. She wondered if Monica would leave her mark on Rayne or if Rayne would let Paul come between them.

Angie took a deep breath. "Well, maybe it would be good if Paul *did* meet her," she said. "Sometimes, when you get to know someone, you find out that she isn't the way people say she is."

Rayne stared at her. "I hadn't thought about it that way," she said. "But I don't know if it would work. Things have gotten so bad between Paul and me that I don't know if anything will *ever* be right again."

The tears brimmed in her eyes and spilled onto her cheeks. "I think it's over between us," she whispered. "And all because Paul is afraid of what people think. And *I* think that's cowardly. Don't you?"

For a moment Angie didn't trust herself to speak. She was close to tears herself. As bad as things were for Monica right now, she didn't know how lucky she was to have a friend like Rayne. *Would my new friends put themselves on the line like that for me in a tough situation?* she wondered. *Would Glenn?*

Angie hoped she would never have to find out.

Chapter Seven

After their talk, Angie and Rayne walked on in silence. Then Lani came up behind them, with her notebook and her tape recorder. She had on a pair of red shorts and a T-shirt that announced ONLY SHE WHO ATTEMPTS THE ABSURD CAN ACHIEVE THE IMPOSSIBLE.

"Hey, where were the elephants?" Rayne demanded, with a look of amusement. "I went outside and looked for them right after breakfast, but they weren't there."

"Yeah, I guess they never showed up," Lani admitted cheerfully. "That's the way it is with safaris. You never know what'll happen."

Angie laughed. She liked Lani's offbeat sense of humor. She glanced at the tape recorder. "How are your interviews coming along?"

Lani gave a nonchalant shrug. "Well, for some reason, the boys all seem to be somewhere else this morning. I mean, when I come up, they just sort of fade into the distance."

Rayne looked at her sideways. "Does that tell you anything?" she asked.

Lani nodded. "I guess so. It tells me that my project is going to bc harder than I thought." Just at that moment, they came around a turn in the path and saw a small sign that said HOWARDS FALLS 1/4 MILE. The side path led up a steep, rocky incline.

Rayne sighed, peering up the cliff. "Why is it that the things you want most to see are always at the end of the steepest paths?"

"That's life, I guess," Lani said.

"Hey, are you guys coming up?" Stephanie peered down at them from the top of the cliff. "It's not very far," she added encouragingly. "And the falls are really worth the climb."

The falls *were* wonderful, Angie decided, after ten minutes of struggling to the top for the view. Standing on a massive wedge of stone, with the cold spray in her face, she silently agreed with Rayne that the best things in life were the hardest to come by. The water cascaded down thirty feet or so, thundering from one rocky ledge to another. The slippery rocks closest to the stream were festooned with green maidenhair fern and clusters of little red, purple, and white flowers, droplets of sparkling spray nestling like diamonds among the leaves.

"Isn't it beautiful?" Stephanie said, coming to stand beside Angie.

Wordlessly, Angie nodded. Somehow, standing here, lost in the roar of the falling water, she felt like a different person. The old Angie, Tony's sister, her father's daughter—that old Angie was back in Glenwood. The Angie who stood here was different. She had the feeling that Stephanie knew exactly how she was feeling.

For a moment, Angie and Stephanie stood there in silence, watching the water tumbling over the cliff. Then a group of kids came up and stood a little distance away, throwing rocks and sticks into the water. Angie glanced at them. There was Glenn, with Shannon close beside him. She winced a little. She had been right. Shannon's hiking outfit *was* color coordinated. She was wearing a pair of hot-pink jogging shorts and a skintight pink V-necked T-shirt. She looked . . . well, *sexy* was the only word for it.

Glenn glanced up and saw Angie and waved. Shannon looked up, too.

"Oh, hi, Angie," she called. "It's really too bad you couldn't come swimming with us last night." She smiled lazily and slipped her arm casually through Glenn's. "We had *such* a good time swimming. Didn't we, Glenn?"

Glenn looked at her for a minute. He didn't seem too unhappy that Shannon was clinging to him, Angie thought. In fact, he seemed to like it. He nodded. "Yeah, it *was* fun," he said.

"In fact," Shannon persisted, "we had such a good time last night that we've decided to do it again tonight." She giggled. "Only this time, we're going skinny-dipping. That *really* ought to be fun."

Angie's heart tumbled down into her shoes. If Glenn and Shannon were going skinny-dipping together, it probably meant that something really serious was going on between them. She tried to smile, but it didn't feel right. She was glad Glenn was too far away to see her expression.

"Hey, look," one of the girls with Shannon called out excitedly. "Look at that bird!"

A bright blue jay suddenly swooped down on a piece of shiny gum foil and carried it, wings flapping noisily, into the pine tree on the other side of the falls. "What kind of bird is that?" the girl asked.

"It's a jay," Glenn said. "They're attracted to bright objects. We used to have one in our back yard, and it was an incorrigible thief. Once it even stole my mom's ring from the picnic table."

"Then it must be what they call a jailbird," Shannon said, with a pointed look at Angie. The other kids laughed uproariously. Even Glenn seemed to be joining in. Was he laughing at *her*?

Angie's face flamed, and she turned away quickly, sucking in a deep breath. Even in this beautiful, out-of-the-way place, where she was beginning to feel like a different person, somebody had to come along and remind her of her reputation.

And even worse, Glenn was probably in on it, too. The thought that Glenn might be laughing at her made Angie feel mad at everyone. Why couldn't they just leave her alone? Suddenly she was seized with the urge to get back at Shannon. But what could she do? How could she get even? She thrust her hands deep into the pockets of her shorts and started off down the rocky path toward the lake, her back and shoulders stiff with frustration and anger.

"Listen, Angie, you've just got to ignore them," Stephanie said, hurrying behind her to catch up. She reached for Angie's arm and jerked her to a stop. "You can't let them see that they've got you. If you do, they'll never let up."

"How would *you* know?" Angie said, bitterly, shaking off Stephanie's hand. "You've never had a brother who's a thief or a father who's a jailbird. People don't continually talk about you behind your back." Burning tears welled up in her eyes, and she brushed them away with the back of her hand.

Stephanie looked at her. "No," she said quietly. "The truth is that I never knew my parents at all. The Enomotos are my foster parents, and Alex isn't really my sister at all."

"Well, maybe you're better off that way," Angie said sadly. "I mean, it's too bad that you don't have a real family and all that. I'm sorry. But at least nobody can come along and take cheap shots at you because of your family's reputation, because of something you didn't have anything to do with in the first place." She turned and started to walk down the path again.

Stephanie fell into step beside her. "No, I guess you're right about that," she admitted, with a crooked smile. "But sometimes people take cheap shots anyway. There was this time that I went on this hike with the Sierra Club . . ." She paused. "But maybe you don't want to hear any more stories."

Angie sighed. "No, tell me," she said dully. Anyway, her hike was ruined—the whole weekend was ruined, for that matter. But she hadn't expected anything better, really, in spite of all her dreams about Glenn St. Clair. So what did it matter if Stephanie wanted to waste her time trying to cheer her up?

Stephanie chuckled. "Well, it didn't seem very

funny at the time, but looking back on it, I can see the humor in it. I went on this hike with the Sierra Club in the Big Sur Mountains, and somehow I got lost. There was this fork in the path, and I went one way, and the rest of the hikers went the other. By the time I realized that I was lost, it was getting dark, and then I twisted my ankle on a loose stone in the path. So I sat down under this big tree."

In spite of herself, Angie felt a stirring of curiosity. "Were you just going to sit there all night?"

"Well, what else could I do?" Stephanie asked reasonably. "The trail was pretty treacherous in the dark, and I didn't know where I was going. And my ankle was really hurting. So I sat down to wait. After a while I heard this rustling in the leaves. For a minute I was really scared. But then I saw a glimmer of light, and I realized that somebody was looking for me. It turned out to be Danny, Alex's boyfriend. By that time, my ankle was really swelling up, so we built this huge fire and we stayed where we were all night."

"Uh-oh," Angie said softly.

"Yeah, right." Stephanie laughed. "A big 'uh-oh.' When we finally got back the next day, Alex was convinced that something had happened between Danny and me, which of course was the last thing on our minds. All we wanted to do was keep warm and get back safe."

"Couldn't you convince her that . . . ?" Angie started to ask.

Stephanie shook her head emphatically. "It wasn't just Alex. It was everybody—all my friends and Alex's too. They all assumed the worst, because . . . well, because I guess I was kind of wild, in those days."

"Wild?"

"Oh, you know," Stephanie said, "I just sort of went out of my way to do outrageous things, just to make people notice me." She laughed a little. "I was the tough kid, the girl who knew all the answers, the girl who would take any dare. But of course, when Alex and the others jumped to conclusions that time with Danny, it made me mad, the way you got mad at Shannon and her friends a minute ago."

"Well, I guess I don't blame you for getting mad," Angie said. "They were saying something about you that you didn't deserve."

They came to the foot of the cliff, where the path from the falls joined the main path. "You know, looking back on it now," Stephanie said thoughtfully, "I'd have to say that a lot of what happened was my own fault."

"I don't understand that," Angie said, frowning. "I don't see how it could have been your fault."

"It was my fault because I had a big chip on my shoulder," Stephanie explained. "I was busy hating the whole human race. All I could think of was how everybody picked on me. And then I would think, well, okay, I'll give them something to *really* talk about. And I'd go and do something stupid to get even—something that I'd regret later." She looked closely at Angie. "It finally dawned on me that nobody was really against me. They were just reacting to the things I was doing. I was my own worst enemy. When I figured that out, things got better in a hurry."

Angie nodded. Suddenly her throat closed up, and she felt like crying. "Thanks, Stephanie," she said.

Stephanie turned and gave her a big hug. "It's going to be okay, Angie," she said fiercely. "Believe me. It will be."

Angie knew what Stephanie was trying to say, and she appreciated the help. But it still didn't change the basic facts. It still didn't change the fact that everybody knew about her family. But still, she had to admit that it was nice to know that Stephanie cared.

The hikers stopped for a picnic lunch on a bluff overlooking the lake. On the opposite side of the lake, in the far distance, they could see the smoke from the lodge, rising up from the trees. To the west, a forbidding cluster of thunderheads loomed against the horizon, and Angie remembered the forecast. It looked like they might get caught in the rain. The dark clouds matched her own unhappy mood.

Mr. Dawson and Ms. Richards, who had been leading the group, had made a campfire, and everybody sat down, pulling out the sandwiches and bags of potato chips that they had brought with them from the lodge that morning. Angie shared a log with Gloria and Tim.

"What a terrific view," Gloria said, unwrapping her sandwich. "You can see all the way across the lake from here." They could see the bright sails of the wind surfers on the lake and on the strip of beach below the lodge, dots of color that must have been beach blankets. "I wish I had some binoculars."

"Isn't that your house?" Tim asked suddenly, pointing.

Gloria looked startled. "Where?" she asked, dropping her sandwich.

"Here, just brush it off," Angie said, picking the sandwich up out of the leaves and handing it to Gloria. "It's only got a few pine needles on it, that's all."

"Over there," Tim said, "on the cliff above the beach. You can see those crazy turrets above the trees."

"Oh," Gloria said. Absently, she brushed the pine needles off her sandwich and took a bite out of it. "Yeah, I guess that's the Belvedere house."

Tim looked at her strangely. "I'd know those turrets anywhere. It's the only house on the lake that looks like it came right out of a fairy tale."

"Right," Gloria said, taking a deep breath.

Angie gave her a sharp look. What was Gloria going to do now?

"That's right," Gloria said again. "A fairy-tale house, complete with Cinderella."

"Huh?" Tim said. He looked confused. "Cinderella? What's *she* got to do with this?"

Gloria looked over at Angie. Angie thought she looked determined, as if she had suddenly decided to tell him. Well, Angie didn't have anything to distract them with this time. She would just have to stay out of it and see what happened.

"Cinderella—you know," Gloria said, "the kitchen maid who got all dressed up to go to the dance, and the prince mistook her for a princess and . . ."

"Hey, what did I tell you, Gloria?" Ginger interrupted. She had come up behind them and put one hand on Gloria's shoulder. "Look." She pointed toward the fire. "They're holding hands."

"Who?" Gloria asked, looking up. "Who's holding hands?" Angie thought that she looked relieved.

Maybe she wasn't ready to tell Tim, after all.

"Mr. Dawson and Ms. Richards, dummy. That's who," Ginger said. "I told you the other day that I thought they'd make a cute couple."

Angie looked. They *were* holding hands. She couldn't help being a little startled. The idea of a biology teacher—especially Ms. Richards—holding hands with somebody seemed a little weird, although she had to admit that Mr. Dawson was a very good-looking man.

Gloria shook her head in bewilderment. "I don't believe it," she said. "The dragon lady holding hands. Wonders will never cease."

Ginger laughed. "Well, they say anything can happen on Orientation Weekend, and I guess they're right."

"Now, what were you saying?" Tim asked Gloria, when Ginger had gone. "Something about Cinderella?"

Gloria was silent for a minute. Then she sighed and shook her head. "I forget," she mumbled.

"I just plain chickened out," Gloria said dejectedly, as she and Angie began to climb the rocks toward the top of the bluff. Lunch was over, and some of the seniors were spending a few minutes climbing around on the rocks before they hiked back to the lodge. "I started to tell him, but I chickened out."

"Were you *really* going to tell him?" Angie asked, pulling herself up over a rocky ledge by grabbing on to a twisted root. "It sounded as if it was sort of accidental."

"No, I guess I didn't really start out to tell him," Gloria admitted breathlessly. She clambered over a big rock. "But then he made that comment about the Belvedere house being like a castle in a fairy tale. I thought of the Cinderella story, and it seemed like maybe I could just sort of back into telling him, instead of coming at it straight on." She shrugged. "It seemed like a good idea at the time. But I have to admit I was glad when Ginger came along and interrupted me."

Angie stepped across to another ledge, trying not to look down. They weren't that far up, but heights made her dizzy. "I'm glad, too," Angie said. "I didn't have any potato salad to dump on Tim's shoe, so I couldn't be of any help. And I didn't think you would want me to smear my peanut-butter-and-jelly sandwich on *your* brand-new sneakers." She hoisted herself up on a big rock, which was still warm from the sun. The rock was crisscrossed by a web of deep, pebble-filled crevices. "Hey, what do you think about Ms. Richards and Mr. Dawson?" she asked idly, poking a stick into one of the crevices.

"I think it's really interesting," Gloria said, climbing onto the ledge above the rock where Angie was sitting. "We'll just have to watch and see what develops. Do you suppose . . ." She glanced back to where Angie was sitting. "Angie!" she screamed frantically. "Angie, don't move!"

"What?" Angie asked, looking up. "What's wrong?"

At that moment Angie heard a sharp, warning buzz, almost like a hissing noise. On the sun-warmed rock to her left, not two feet away, lay an enormous coiled rattlesnake, head pulled back, tongue flicking in and out.

For a second, Angie stared at the snake. "Oh, God," she whispered, fear seizing her in a cold, hard clutch.

"Don't move, Angie," Gloria begged from her perch. "If you move, it'll strike!"

"I *can't* move," Angie whispered, staring at the snake, its cold, amber-colored eyes seeming to hold hers in icy fascination. She couldn't pull her eyes away from it, even though the sight of it made her head swim. "Gloria, I . . . I can't move at all!"

Chapter Eight

The deadly fear seemed to paralyze Angie's arms and legs, and even her lungs seemed to be caught in a horrible vise. But she was shivering uncontrollably. Although the sun was warm on her back, she felt icy cold. "I can't move!" she whispered again, panic rising in her like a cold fog.

"Hold still for a minute or two," she heard a warm, soothing voice say. "Everything will be fine. Just don't look. Close your eyes. Okay?"

At the sound of Glenn's quiet voice, Angie suddenly found she could breathe again. Obediently, she squeezed her eyes shut. Then she heard the loud, solid thud of a rock. When she opened her eyes, the snake was lying limply against the rock, dead.

In a quick move, Glenn jumped over to where Angie was sitting. "Are you okay?" he asked. He pulled her to her feet and put his arm around her.

Angie took a deep breath. The sudden shock of relief was so intense that she felt dizzy, and the strength drained from her legs. There was a loud roaring in her ears, and she sagged limply against Glenn's arm.

"Hey, you'd better sit down," Glenn said, his voice sounding concerned. "You look a little pale." He lowered her gently to a sitting position and began to rub her hands. "Are you okay?" he asked again.

"I think so," Angie said, after a moment, leaning weakly against the rocks. The dizziness was fading, and her hands felt warmer with Glenn holding them.

"Oh, Angie," Gloria said anxiously, scrambling down to the ledge. "I thought you were going to be killed!"

She paused, looking knowingly at the two of them. "Well, I guess I'll just go on down and see if I can find Tim."

"Thanks, Gloria," Angie said. "If you hadn't yelled at me . . ." She shivered.

"Don't mention it," Gloria said, starting down.

"And I guess I ought to thank you, too, Glenn," Angie said in a low voice. "Killing the rattlesnake was a very brave thing to do." The flood of gratitude she felt toward Glenn warmed her, and she stopped shivering.

"No big deal," Glenn said briskly, straightening up. "It was just something that had to be done. You would have done it, if you'd had to." He pushed the snake into a crevice with his foot and covered it over with pebbles.

"No, I couldn't have," Angie said, shaking her head emphatically. "I wouldn't have known how to do it. I was lucky that you were around."

Glenn sat down again next to Angie. "I learned about snakes from my grandfather," he said. "He was a prospector—one of those old guys who was never lucky enough to strike it rich but who never gave up hope. When I was a kid, I used to spend summers with him in the mountains, looking for the mother lode. He was a scruffy old dude who never amounted to very much because he refused to give up his wandering ways and settle down and get civilized. But I loved him, and I learned a lot from him. Those summers were the best times of my life. Sometimes we wouldn't see another soul for two months. We ate beans and salt pork and beef jerky and lived in his mountain cabin. It was great."

Angie shook her head, smiling a little. "Somehow it doesn't fit my image of you," she said, thinking about the Glenn she had known at school. "I mean, it's a little hard to imagine the student body president living for the summer on beans and salt pork and beef jerky."

Glenn gave Angie a steady look. "There's a lot about me you don't know. When my father was a little boy, he and my grandfather lived in a hard-luck shanty on the edge of the desert." He laughed a little. "Dad says that he can remember being so poor and hungry that even the rattlesnakes looked good to eat."

Angie stared at Glenn. "I thought your dad was a lawyer, with his own firm. I thought that your family had lots of money."

"Sure, we do now," Glenn said, looking out over the lake. "My parents have what they want, and so do I. But that's because my father was determined. He worked hard to get a scholarship to a good college. He pushed himself. He wanted to do something more with his life than pan streams looking for gold, hoping to get lucky." He paused reflectively. "I guess that's why he's always leaning on me about getting good grades and being a leader. He wants *me* to amount to something on my own, the way he did. He's always saying it's not how you start that counts, it's how you finish. In his life, that really means something."

It's not how you start but how you finish. For a

minute, Angie sat quietly, thinking about what Glenn had said. For most of her life, she had thought it was the way you *started* that made the difference. She had started life as a Maroni, with three strikes against her—well, two, anyway—and sometimes, when things didn't turn out, no matter how hard she tried, she felt that was exactly how she was going to finish. She wasn't ever going to be anything more than she was now. But Glenn was saying that that wasn't true. It was something for her to remember.

"Listen, Angie, there's something else I wanted to tell you," Glenn said in a low voice, looking down at his hands. "It wasn't any accident that I was close by a few minutes ago—close enough to kill the snake."

"It wasn't?"

"No. I was looking for you, and somebody said you had climbed up here. I wanted to talk to you—about this morning."

"This morning?" After the excitement of the past few minutes, the morning seemed like a million years ago.

"Yeah, about what Shannon said at the falls." He reached down and retied the shoelace of his sneaker. "—About that bird."

Angie was silent for a moment. Then she said lamely, "Yes, I remember."

Glenn squared his shoulders and looked at her.

"Well, I want you to know that I didn't know about your father when I was telling the kids about the jay in our backyard—about the jay stealing Mom's ring, I mean."

"You didn't know?" Angie asked incredulously. "I thought *everybody* knew about my father—and my brother, too."

Glenn shook his head. "Nope. In fact, I doubt if very many people know about them at all—or care as much as you think they do. Most people are too busy worrying about themselves to worry about other people." He frowned. "But after Shannon told me about your father and your brother, I got really mad—mad at *her* for making such a stupid remark. I'm really sorry about the whole thing."

Angie smiled. She felt so happy, she had to stop herself from shouting for joy. "Well, you just saved my life. So I think we're even."

Glenn grinned at her. "Okay, I accept that," he said. "Even stephen." He held out his hand and pulled her to her feet. "Think you can negotiate the climb down? I'll help."

Angie nodded. The way she felt now, she could climb Mt. Everest!

When Angie and Glenn climbed down from the cliff, they found that most of the hikers had already taken the trail back to the lodge. The rest of the hike, for Angie, was a journey through sheer paradise. It didn't matter at all that the thunderclouds still loomed in the west, or that her feet felt pinched and blistered in Gloria's shoes. For her, the birds in the trees sang sweeter, the fragrance of the pine needles was fresher and sharper, and the breeze was softer—and all because Glenn St. Clair was walking shoulder-to-shoulder with her down the path, sharing the hike with her.

They loafed along, in no particular hurry, spending the time telling each other about their lives. Glenn told Angie about growing up lonely as an only child. He talked about how proud he was of his mother, who had gone back to college several years ago and had graduated from San Francisco State last year with honors. Now she was studying law at Stanford.

"I really admire her," he added. "She didn't *have* to go back to school, but she wanted to do something more than go to afternoon teas at the Garden Club or manage volunteers for the church. She thinks it's important to have an independent life of her own, apart from my dad's, and I think it's great."

When it was Angie's turn to talk, she found that Glenn was a good listener, asking exactly the right questions at the right time. It was funny, but his ability to listen made it a lot easier for her to talk, and she found herself telling him things that she'd never told anybody else—things about her family, about her father, about her brother.

"The night that Tony was arrested was the worst of all," she said. "The police came and got him, and Mom and my little sisters were crying. But he didn't seem to care, somehow. He just acted tougher than ever, as if it didn't matter how much it hurt the rest of us."

Glenn was silent for a minute. "Well, I guess everybody has a different way of dealing with being hurt, but I'll bet that Tony was hurting, too. He just managed to cover it up better than the rest of you."

Angie stared at him. "Do you think so?"

"I don't have any way to prove it," Glenn admitted. "But he had to have felt *some* kind of hurt. Tough guys can't cry, you know. It's against the rules."

Talking to Glenn made Angie feel so much better. The hurt of the morning seemed to be washed away by his kindness and attention. It didn't seem to matter what she told him, he accepted it all. And although she was exhausted, she was disappointed when the lodge suddenly loomed up through the trees ahead. It meant that her perfect afternoon with Glenn was coming to an end.

"There you are," Gloria said with relief in her voice, as Angie and Glenn reached the front porch of the lodge. "I was beginning to get worried about you. I thought we'd have to send out a search party." She pointed at Lani, who was with her. "Lani had already volunteered to round up her elephants and start out."

"Listen, it's been great, Angie," Glenn said. "I guess I'd better get back to my cabin." He waved casually. "See you later."

"Okay," Angie said, feeling let down. "See you later." She had hoped that he would ask her to go with him to the wiener roast that night on the beach. But that was asking a lot, she reminded herself. Just because he made an effort to apologize for Shannon and wound up walking her back to the lodge didn't mean that he was interested in her.

Just then, Stephanie came around the corner, carrying a heavy rope. "Everybody ready for the tug-of-war?" she asked. "I hope you guys are really feeling strong this afternoon."

"Tug-of-war?" Lani echoed. "Hey, that sounds like fun. Where are we having it?"

"Down on the beach," Stephanie said. "It looks like it's not going to rain after all. Why don't you put on your bathing suits and meet us down there. The guys are digging a big pit in the sand. We're going to fill it with water, and the cabins are going to compete against one another."

Angie and Gloria hurried to the cabin. Angie wasn't very happy about wearing her blue bathing suit. It was at least two years old and had begun to fade. But if she wore a shirt over it, it would do.

Rayne was already at the cabin, lying on her bed. She was facing the wall and had a pillow pulled over her head.

"Hey, Rayne, are you all right?" Angie said, sitting on the edge of the cot. She put a hand on Rayne's shoulder.

Rayne pushed the pillow away and turned over. Her eyes were red from crying, and her cheeks were blotchy and stained with tears. "No, I'm not all right," she said.

"Did you and Paul have another argument?"

"Not another one. Just a repeat of the *same* one, that's all." She rubbed her eyes. "What are you doing here?"

"We came to get our bathing suits for the tug-of-war," Gloria said. "Come on, get up. You have to come, too. We won't stand a chance without everybody pulling their weight."

"I don't want to," Rayne said, with a self-pitying sigh. She rolled back over toward the wall. "I'd rather stay here by myself."

Gloria looked at Angie with a raised eyebrow. Angie nodded slightly. Together, they grabbed Rayne and dragged her out of the bunk. Gloria pulled her sweat shirt off while Angie pulled her shorts down. In a moment, she was sitting on the floor, shivering, stripped to her bra and panties. Lani fished in Rayne's luggage and pulled out her bikini.

"Okay, Rayne," Lani said, dangling the bikini by one of its straps. "It's time to get dressed. Our cabin is going to win that tug-of-war!"

Rayne laughed in spite of herself. "I guess you won't take no for an answer," she said.

"Yes, we won't take no for an answer," Lani said.

"Now all we have to do is find Nancy," Gloria said.

"Somebody looking for me?" Nancy asked, coming in the door.

"Super!" Lani crowed, clasping her hands over her head and whistling the theme music from *Rocky*.

Everybody was gathered down on the beach, where the boys had dug a big six-foot-square pit in the sand. They had filled it with sand and dirt and water until it was sloshy and muddy.

"What's the mud for?" Angie asked, as they stood looking at it.

"Haven't you ever been in a *real* tug-of-war before?" Stephanie asked, coming up with Elaine.

Stephanie had a whistle around her neck.

Angie shook her head. "No, just the kind we have in gym class where we try to pull people across the center line of the floor."

"Well, this is a *gen-u-ine* tug-of-war," Stephanie explained, with a grin. "The pit is for the losers. It's the booby prize. The winners are the ones who can drag the losers into the mud."

"What do the winners get?" Gloria wanted to know.

"Are you kidding?" Elaine asked. "The winners get to stay clean. Isn't that enough of a prize in itself?"

"Oh, gosh," Nancy said, patting her hair. "I don't know if this is such a good idea. That mud looks pretty awful. And I just washed my hair."

"Well, we just have to win, that's all," Gloria said, casting a worried look at the pit. "The mud is a pretty strong incentive."

"After the tug-of-war," Elaine told them, "there's a belly-flop contest off the dock."

Nancy patted her hair again. "Oh, great," she muttered. "Can't we do *anything* where you don't get either all muddy or all wet?"

"Nothing that really matters," Lani said, with an intelligent look. "Remember what Confucius says?"

Nancy sighed resignedly. "No, Lani, we don't remember what Confucius says. But no doubt you're going to tell us."

"No doubt," Lani agreed. "Confucius says that you never get anywhere in life unless you're willing to get your hair wet." She giggled and ran off, ducking the handful of sand that Nancy threw at her.

Pairs of cabins lined up on either side of the pit, girls against girls, boys against boys, and the competition began. There was a great deal of noisy excitement as the stronger group tugged the weaker one, shouting and clamoring, into the muddy pit, while everybody else stood on the sidelines, jumping up and down and loudly cheering on their favorites.

Angie watched while Glenn's cabin, with Glenn in front, pulled another cabin into the mud. When they had won, Glenn gave her a thumbs-up sign and a triumphant grin.

"Not bad for a bunch of amateurs, huh?" he called across the sand.

"Way to go," said Angie laughing. "You made it look easy. Can we hire you as a consultant when it's our turn?"

"Oh, Glenn, that was simply wonderful," Shannon cooed, rushing up to him and throwing her arms around his neck. Shannon's skimpy black bikini was *very* revealing, Angie noticed. It showed every curve of her body and a great deal of tanned skin. "You're *so* strong."

Glenn looked down at Shannon for a minute and then coolly pulled her arms away. "Thanks," he said casually. "It's always good to know you have a fan club."

As Glenn turned away, Angie caught a spiteful glare from Shannon. It was obvious that she was blaming Angie for Glenn's coolness.

"Okay, gang, it's our turn," Lani said, motioning everybody from the cabin to gather on one side of the pit. "Think positive!"

Gloria shaded her eyes and looked across the pit. "Who are our opponents?" she asked. "Uh-oh, it's Shannon Welles's cabin. And they've got Olga Petrovic!"

"Olga Petrovic!" Nancy echoed. She looked up. "Oh, no! Listen, you guys, you've got to help me keep my hair out of the mud."

"Who's Olga Petrovic?" Lani asked.

"Just look," Rayne said, with a groan. "You can't miss her. She's the one with the bulging biceps. I hear she lifts weights." She shook her head. "I knew I should have worn my old bathing suit. I'd hate to get mud all over this one."

Lani looked. The girls from Shannon's cabin were lining up across the pit, holding on to the rope. Shannon was first, just on the other side of the pit, and at the end of the rope was a tall, stocky girl. She looked *very* muscular in her brown tank suit.

"Olga is Glenwood's champion track star," Rayne explained to Lani. "The shot put is her best event."

"Yeah," Nancy added, "and her nickname is the 'Hulk.'"

"Oh," Lani said, in a small voice. "I see."

"Well, come on, everybody," Rayne said enthusiastically. "We haven't been beaten yet! Grab the rope and hang on! Give it all you've got!"

Standing beside the pit, Stephanie blew her whistle, and the two cabins began to pull. Angie was first, directly across from Shannon, and she could see the wicked gleam in Shannon's eyes. She even thought she could feel the power of her dislike surging through the rope. For a few moments, it seemed as if the two groups were evenly matched, and they seesawed back and forth, with a great deal of shouting from the crowd.

"Way to go, Gloria!" Tim called.

"Hang in there, you guys!" Paul Mitchell shouted.

"Go for it, Angie," Glenn said encouragingly. She realized that he was standing almost at her elbow, and that gave her new strength. She pulled as hard as she could.

But it wasn't hard enough. After a few moments, she could feel herself being slowly tugged forward;

and even though she dug her heels into the sand and leaned all her weight backward, it was no use. There was just too much weight on the other end of the rope.

"We're losing it!" Nancy screamed, behind her.

"Don't give up yet, gang," Lani gasped. "Come on, pull!"

"It's no use," Rayne cried, as they were dragged forward, inch by inch, toward the muddy pit.

"Oh, God," Gloria moaned. "Why did it *have* to be Olga?"

Across the pit, Angie could hear Shannon's triumphant laugh. "Okay, now let's see how a muddy Maroni looks," Shannon taunted. And then Angie and the others lost their footing and were tugged, screaming and laughing, toward the muddy pit.

Chapter Nine

"You know, I think it was pretty smart of Lani to remember the belly flop contest," Gloria remarked, as she and Angie came out of the girls' showers and headed across the lawn toward the cabin. "The rest of us were in no condition to remember anything, after that disastrous tug-of-war." In fact, all Gloria could remember was sliding feetfirst into the pit with a huge, muddy splash, and then mud up her nose, in her ears, in her eyes. Talk about humiliating!

"Right," Angie agreed, soberly. "All I can remember is Shannon jumping up and down and hugging everybody and laughing. If it hadn't been for Lani, we would have gone on feeling terrible for the rest of the day."

"Listen, you guys," Lani had said. They were all

huddled together after climbing out of the mud, bedraggled and shivering. "Don't give up. There's still hope."

"Hope for what?" Nancy moaned, pulling a glob of muddy sand out of her hair. "A nice hot shower? A nap?"

"Nope," Lani said triumphantly. "A belly flop!"

"Come on," Gloria had said with disgust. "You've got to be kidding, Lani." How could she even *think* about the belly flop contest at this horrible moment?

"No, I'm not kidding," Lani had insisted. "Listen, we'll all run down to the dock holding hands, call ourselves the Filthy Five, and do one gigantic belly flop. All together. If nothing else, we'll get the prize for the most ingenious costumes." She looked at Angie, dripping mud from head to toe, and giggled. "The latest in all-over mud."

Rayne looked at the others. "Well, we've got to get this mud off one way or another," she said shrugging. "Maybe Lani's got a good idea. What have we got to lose?"

And that's what they had done. The five of them together, holding hands, had jumped off the end of the dock, sending an enormous splash towering high into the air. Craig, who was running the belly flop contest, had announced them the winners immediately, to the great glee of the crowd. Gloria had to admit that Lani's idea *had* been a good one.

Now, showered and hair washed, Gloria and Angie were on their way back to the cabin to get ready for tonight's wiener roast. The sun was setting behind a sea of deep-red clouds, the same thunderclouds that had been looming in the west all afternoon.

"Do you think it's going to rain tonight?" Angie asked, as they went into the cabin.

"Probably." Gloria sighed, thinking about what she was going to wear. "I've just got my hair the way I want it, so it'll probably pour when we're out on the beach."

"What are you wearing to the wiener roast?" Nancy asked. She was sitting on her bunk, looking at a tear in a pair of rumpled khaki shorts. "Does anybody have a needle and thread?"

"Oh, jeans and a T-shirt, I guess," Gloria decided. She fished in her luggage and found a sewing kit for Nancy. "It might be a little cool out there tonight, especially with a storm coming up." She sighed unhappily. "Actually, I'm more worried about what I'm going to wear *tomorrow* night. I don't have anything that I really feel good about wearing to the dance." The truth of the matter was that the dress she had originally planned on wearing seemed too ordinary now. If she were really as wealthy as Tim thought she was, she would have some kind of fancy designer dress for the occasion. She looked from one to the other. "What are you guys wearing?"

After Gloria had seen the dresses the other girls planned to wear, she felt even more unhappy. Nancy and Lani had brand-new dresses, Rayne was wearing a stylish pair of black velvet pants with a silk chemise top, and Angie had borrowed a party dress from her sister. "Well, that settles it," Gloria said finally, thinking about the balance in her checking account—the money that was supposed to go toward her college fund. "I have to go into town and go shopping tomorrow. I've got to find something really special to wear."

"Town?" Nancy asked curiously, holding up her mended shorts for inspection. "Is there a *town* around here? I thought we were out in the woods."

Gloria laughed. "Of course there's a town. You don't have an exclusive resort like this one without a town somewhere close by. Lakeway is about five miles away, and there's a mall there. I can probably borrow one of the Belvederes' cars. Anybody want to go with me?" she asked.

"Are we allowed to just leave like that?" Nancy asked.

"Oh, I forgot," Gloria said. "I'm just so used to running into town for the Belvederes. But I could probably get permission since technically I'm still working for them. I'll ask Ms. Richards if you can come with me."

"Well I'm conducting interviews tomorrow morning," Lani said.

"And Glenn said he'd show me how to wind surf tomorrow," Angie chimed in.

"I wish I could go with you," Rayne said. "Paul and I seem to keep running into each other, and I'd love to get away for a while."

Gloria turned to Nancy. "Speaking of running into each other, wasn't that Dave Carstairs I saw you with this afternoon, after the belly flop contest?" Gloria had noticed Nancy and Dave together watching the volleyball game.

Nancy's face flamed, and she looked away. "What of it?" she asked defensively.

"Well, aren't you the girl who swore off love just yesterday?" Gloria teased, with a half smile. "Or have I got you mixed up with somebody else?"

"Love has nothing to do with Dave Carstairs and me," Nancy said frostily. She climbed into her shorts. "We were talking business, that's all."

"Must have been pretty interesting business," Lani chimed in. "You two really had your heads together."

"Well, if you *must* know," Nancy said, "we were

talking about *The Glenwood Call.* After all, we *are* going to be working together on the paper next year. We were talking about ideas for feature stories and things like that." She shrugged into a clean blouse. "My general opinion about boys remains exactly the same as it was yesterday," she added somberly. "They are all out to get just as much as they can, from as many different girls as they can. They'll use all the tricks in the book to make you fall in love with them, and then they'll throw you over for somebody else, just for fun."

"My research doesn't bear that out, you know," Lani said earnestly, bending over to tie her shoelaces. "In fact, I've been surprised. The boys I've talked to who take the questions seriously say that they want somebody they can trust—somebody they can count on. They seem to believe that it's the *girl* who uses all the tricks in the book to make a guy fall in love with her. And then she dumps him for somebody else."

"Really?" Gloria asked. She pulled on her Glenwood High sweat shirt. "Have you interviewed Tim yet? What did *he* say?"

Lani grinned and shook her head. "Sorry, Gloria. A true researcher doesn't reveal the sources of her data. You have to protect the anonymity of the informants."

Gloria stared at her. "'Protect the anonymity of the informants?' What is this? A research project or a police procedure?" Realizing how sensitive Angie must be on the subject of police, Gloria immediately regretted her thoughtless remark. She threw a quick glance at Angie. Would she be offended?

Angie laughed. "It's okay, Gloria. My skin is a little thicker today."

Lani gave Gloria an exasperated look. "You're thinking of an informer, Gloria," she said stiffly, picking up her tape recorder and slinging it over her shoulder. "The word *informant* refers to a person who provides important information to a researcher. In order for a research project to be valid, the information that the informants give has to be kept secret. Otherwise, the data might be contaminated."

Laughing, Gloria heaved a pillow at her. "Boy, are you in for it next year," she promised. "We're going to make sure that your senior year is a year you will *never* forget!"

Lani grinned and gathered up her notebook. "You know," she said, "You guys make me feel really *normal.* For the first time in my life."

"Normal?" Gloria asked. She glanced at Lani's tape recorder, adding with a good-natured laugh, "You're taking a tape recorder to a wiener roast, and you talk about *normal*?"

When Gloria and the others arrived on the beach, there was a huge bonfire blazing away in a deep pit in the sand. Nearby, Ginger and Craig had set up a table loaded with hot dogs, buns, relishes, chips, and marshmallows. The boys had cut dozens of willow wands to use for hot dog sticks, and everybody was in charge of roasting their own.

Gloria found herself a place beside the fire where she could roast a hot dog without burning it and settled down on the sand. In the distance, there was a jagged flicker of lightning and a growl of thunder.

"Is this seat saved?" Tim asked, pointing to the sand beside her.

Gloria's heart leaped the way it always did when she saw Tim. "Of course it's saved," she answered warmly, "for you."

"I've managed to get tomorrow off," Tim said, as he squatted on his heels and turned his hot dog over the red-hot coals. "How about going sailing with me? We could take one of the little Fireballs and sail over to the island for a picnic."

"That would be wonderful!" Gloria exclaimed. But then she remembered the dance and the trip she'd planned for the next day. With everyone else all dressed up for the dance, Tim would expect her to be wearing something extraspecial. "But I can't," she said. "I...I've got to go into town and do some shopping."

Tim was silent for a minute. "That's too bad," he said quietly. "I was kind of counting on it. It would have been fun." He turned his hot dog over. "Well, why don't we plan on spending a whole weekend sailing sometime during September? After all, I imagine that you come up here pretty regularly, even during the off-season."

Gloria cleared her throat. "Yes, pretty often." Well, she probably *could*, anyway. The Belvederes would be coming a couple of times a month, and they would want somebody to watch the twins. Of course, that wasn't exactly what Tim meant.

Tim slipped his hot dog into a bun and began to eat. "You know, it's going to be a great senior year, better than I imagined," he said with a satisfied grin. "You can show me all around Glenwood, and we can spend some weekends up here. And the way Mother and Dad have it planned, our families will get to know one another, too. What could be better?"

"Right," Gloria echoed tonelessly. "What could be better?" She sat staring at the fire. *What could be worse?* She knew that Tim cared for her as much as she cared for him. But what were the chances that he would still feel the same after he found out that she wasn't related to the Belvederes? When he found out that her parents were just ordinary people, the kind who ate cornflakes for breakfast and for whom catching a movie at the local theater was a night on the town.

Even if Tim was able to accept the fact that her family didn't have money, how could he ever forgive her for lying to him?

"Hey!" Tim said, sitting up and putting his arm around her. "How come you're so gloomy tonight? Come on—smile, Gloria. We've got a lot to be happy about."

Gloria leaned back into the warm curve of his arm and watched the sparks fly upward. She couldn't tell him now and wreck this wonderful weekend. All she had to do was get through tonight and tomorrow and tomorrow night—and then she would tell him on Sunday. All she had to do was pretend just a little while longer. She sighed. "Oh, yes," she said. "We have a lot to be happy about." *At least for a little while*, she added to herself.

Angie sat all alone on a log she had pulled up beside the fire, roasting her hot dog and feeling the flames hot on her face. Then Nancy came over to sit beside her, and the two of them ate in a companionable silence.

"I don't think she ought to be doing what she's doing," Nancy said suddenly.

"Who?" Angie asked in confusion. "Doing what?"

"Gloria," Nancy said, pointing to where Gloria and Tim were lying together talking, feet stretched toward the fire. "She ought to tell him."

"Don't you think she will?"

"It doesn't look like it," Nancy stated matter-of-factly. She looked in the other direction. "How can you have a real relationship based on lies?" She sounded as if she were going to cry, and Angie found herself reaching out for her hand.

"But Gloria didn't *intentionally* deceive him," Angie objected.

"Maybe not, but in my book, if you let somebody think something that isn't true, you're deceiving him, just the same as if you'd lied to him." She swallowed hard. "It's just like what happened to me this summer with that guy I told you about. He never told me he had a girl friend back home." She was silent for a moment, and then she went on. "Maybe he didn't exactly *lie* to me, but he deceived me, all the same. And it hurt, a lot. I'll never trust another boy again. And I don't want to see the same thing happen to Gloria and Tim."

"Yes, but it's not the same thing," Angie objected. "This is just a misunderstanding, and it'll soon get straightened out. And anyway, Tim didn't tell Gloria the truth, either—about his family owning the resort, I mean. So they're sort of even."

"Not the way I see it," Nancy insisted. She paused. "The whole thing is really bothering me. I'm going to talk to her about it when we go shopping tomorrow. Maybe I can convince her to stop putting it off."

In the distance, Angie could hear the rattle of thunder, and a flicker of lightning crackled through the air.

Suddenly Dave Carstairs stepped up beside the fire. "Hey, you girls had better keep an eye on Lani Connors," he said, sitting down on the log beside Nancy. He was frowning. "I'm afraid she's going to get herself in trouble again."

Nancy looked up. "What kind of trouble can she get herself into—besides *mouth* trouble."

"That's exactly the kind of trouble I'm talking about," Dave said. "Look." He pointed to the other side of the fire, where Lani stood with her microphone and tape recorder. "She hasn't touched a hot dog, as far as I can see. But she's been roasting Darryl Howe for the past ten minutes."

"Look," Darryl was saying as he backed away from Lani, both hands up, "I don't care *how* many guys have answered your stupid questions. I'm not going to tell you another thing. And that's all there is to it."

"What do you have against girls?" Lani asked in a

reasonable tone, following him as he backed away and continuing to hold the microphone up to his mouth. "I mean, have you had a romance go sour, or something like that? Is that why you won't answer my questions?"

Darryl shook his head. "No," he muttered defensively, taking another step backward. "Nothing like that. I . . . I just don't want to, that's all."

"Well, then, what are you afraid of?" Lani asked. "They're just questions, that's all. It's no big deal."

"It *is* a big deal," Darryl roared suddenly. "You're invading my privacy!" All around them, people stopped talking and eating and looked up, but Darryl didn't seem to notice. "I mean, people don't want their private lives to be the subject of somebody's research, for Pete's sake!" There was scattered applause from the crowd as Darryl turned and stalked away.

Nancy sighed. "Has that been going on all evening?"

Dave nodded. "Yeah, I'm afraid so. As long as I've been watching, anyway." He turned to the girls with a smile. "Looks like drastic action is called for."

Angie leaned forward to look past Nancy at Dave. She had an idea. "Will you help?" she asked.

Dave shrugged. "Well, sure," he said. "But I don't know what I can do."

Angie explained her idea.

"I don't know if that'll work," Nancy said, frowning and shaking her head. "What if it makes her mad?"

"What's the alternative?" Dave asked with a shrug. "Tying her up and gagging her and locking her in the cabin?" He nodded at Angie. "I'm ready," he said, "anytime you are."

"Okay," Angie said. She scrambled to her feet. "Let's go."

The three of them went around the fire to where Lani was zeroing in on her next victim, a tall redheaded boy with horn-rimmed glasses who was beginning to look a little apprehensive.

"Hey, Lani," Dave said casually, going up to her. "Do you have a minute?"

"Sure," Lani said, momentarily abandoning the redheaded boy. "What's on your mind?"

"You know, I've had second thoughts about doing that interview. If you still want me to, I'd be willing to answer your questions."

"Really?" Lani asked eagerly. "Gosh, that's terrific, Dave." She turned to the redheaded boy, who was rapidly edging away. "Listen, Michael, don't go away. Okay? I'll get back to you as soon as I can. I really do want to talk to you."

"Oh, sure," the boy muttered. "Sure thing." And he scuttled off into the darkness with a look of intense relief on his face.

Dave gestured toward a gently sloping sand dune in the shadows beyond the fire. "Let's go sit over there, where nobody's going to bother us," he said. He led her into the darkness, still talking, while Angie and Nancy circled surreptitiously behind the dune and crept up to the top, trying not to make any noise.

"Just let me get this tape changed before we start," Lani said, fumbling with her recorder. "It's my last one. I'll have to ask Gloria to get me some more when she goes to town tomorrow." Angie could hear the rattle of the cassette as Lani replaced it in the tape recorder. "There. Now, we can get started," Lani said. "The first thing I want to know is . . ."

"*Aaaaaarrrrgggh!* It's a stick-up!" Angie and Nancy shouted in unison, jumping over the top of the dune. "Hands up, everybody! Give us your goodies!"

"I don't *have* any goodies," Dave said mildly, raising his hands in the air. "I don't even have my watch on." He opened his mouth very wide. "However, I do have one or two gold fillings, if you insist."

"What?" Lani cried, jumping up. "Come on, you guys, you're interrupting. What kind of stupid joke is this?"

Nancy put her hands on Lani's shoulders and

pushed her back down. "It's no stupid joke, it's a stupid stick-up," she said. "This is highway robbery." Suddenly she giggled. "Well, beach-front robbery, maybe."

"Can't you girls go play your games somewhere else?" Lani inquired in a tone of irritation. "Can't you see that what we're doing has real scientific significance? It's *research*."

"Right," Angie said, "research with real scientific significance. I *knew* we were on the trail of something important!" She reached for Lani's tape recorder and unsnapped the cassette. "Actually, this is all we need." She put the cassette into the pocket of her jeans. "Okay, everybody, holdup's over."

Dave put his hands down with a grin. "You don't want my fillings? Gosh, my mother's going to be glad to hear that. They cost a bundle."

"Hey!" Lani said indignantly, reaching for the cassette. Angie danced away. "If you take that tape, I can't conduct any more interviews tonight. It's the only one I have left!"

"Exactly, my dear Watson," Nancy said smoothly. "How clever of you. Lani, my friend, we are saving you from yourself. Nobody wants to answer questions tonight. They want to eat hot dogs and marshmallows and enjoy the fire." She paused. "And now that you can't use your mouth to talk into your tape recorder, how about using it to eat? You must be starving by now."

For a minute, Angie wasn't sure whether Lani was going to be mad or join in the joke. Then she suddenly broke down into a convulsion of giggles. "You guys are something else," she gasped.

Chapter Ten

"I saw that," Glenn said, sitting down on the log next to Angie and stretching his hands toward the fire. A chilly breeze had sprung up off the lake.

"Saw what?" Still buried in her thoughts, Angie looked up in surprise from the marshmallow she was toasting over the flames. "What did you see?"

"What you and Nancy Colton and Dave Carstairs did to Lani Connors," Glenn said. "She was really getting to be a pain—and look at her now." He pointed. "Why, there might be a human being attached to that scientific brain of hers, after all."

Angie looked. Lani and Nancy and Dave Carstairs were sitting together beside the fire with Mr. Dawson and Ms. Richards. They were all laughing.

Angie giggled. "Oh, she's human, all right," she

said, turning her attention back to her marshmallow. "And she knows how to take a joke, even when it's on her."

"Yeah," Glenn said reflectively, "I guess that's a pretty tough assignment." He looked at Angie. "Listen, it was a nice day. The hike and all, I mean."

"Yes, it was," Angie agreed. She took a bite of the marshmallow and offered the rest to Glenn. "Especially the part where you killed the snake." She shivered a little, remembering it.

"Well I wasn't thinking about that so much as about later, when we were walking back together," Glenn said, licking his sticky fingers and staring into the fire. "I just really enjoyed talking to you."

At that moment, Paul Mitchell, on the other side of Angie, picked up his guitar and began to play a soft, haunting melody. Rayne was sitting next to him, and it looked to Angie as though the two of them were making a concerted effort not to touch each other. But as Paul began to sing in a strong tenor voice, Rayne joined in with her lovely soprano. Angie, remembering what Rayne had told her only that morning, could hear the ache in her voice as she sang. Would Rayne and Paul ever settle the trouble between them? She hoped that they would. It was pretty obvious that they loved each other, and it just didn't make sense that Rayne's friendship with Monica could come between them.

When the first song was over, Paul started to play "Puff the Magic Dragon," and Angie joined in with her deep alto, at first very quietly, and then with greater assurance. It was one of her favorites, a song she remembered from her childhood. The others around the fire fell silent as she and Paul and Rayne sang together in a soft, lilting harmony. When they had finished the last verse, there was quiet applause and calls for "more, more." But Paul put down the guitar and, with only a brief nod for Rayne and a smile for Angie, left the fire. Rayne stared after him with a look of such utter devastation on her face that Angie shivered. And then, suddenly, with a strangled sob, she scrambled to her feet and darted off in the opposite direction from Paul.

Angie started to get up to go after her, but Glenn was talking. "You have a *terrific* voice, Angie," he was saying, with interest. "Do you do any performing?"

Angie shook her head, settling back into place. She would try to console Rayne later. Right now she wanted to stay with Glenn. She had a feeling that Rayne would understand. "No, I've never done much serious singing," she said. "Except for school chorus, that is. I sang in *The Pirates of Penzance* last year. And sometimes I sing with my brother. He plays guitar in a band, and when they practice at our house, I sit in with them. I... well, maybe someday I'll be good enough to..."

At that moment, there was a flash of nearby lightning and a sudden crash of thunder. Angie jumped, and Glenn put his arm around her. "Hey, it's only thunder," he said.

"Yeah, I know," Angie said, with a little laugh. She shivered. "It startled me, that's all." A splatter of fat raindrops hissed into the fire.

"Come on, we're going to get wet," Glenn exclaimed. "Let's run for it!" And they dashed up the beach toward the lodge, with the rest of the kids.

The rain that had threatened all day turned into a sudden, drenching downpour, dousing the bonfire immediately and turning it into a heap of steamy ashes. For a few minutes, everybody clustered noisily on the porch, trying to decide what to do. Then some people ran for the cabins, while others went into the lodge to watch television or play games. Angie and Glenn sat for a long time, perched comfortably on the porch rail, not saying anything, just watching the lightning play over the lake and listening to the crackle of the thunder.

Then, behind her, Angie heard, "There they are!" in a loud whisper. It sounded like Shannon's voice. Someone else said, in a normal tone, "Oh, don't worry, Shannon. I'm sure Angie is more interested in stealing Glenn's *wallet* than she is in stealing *him* from you."

Angie stiffened. For a moment she hesitated. Most of all, she wanted to turn around and scream at them, tell them that she had nothing to do with her family's reputation—tell them that she was her *own* person, with her own set of values and her own code of conduct. But then the familiar hopelessness set in. What good would it do? As Stephanie had said, people would believe whatever they wanted to believe.

Without looking around, she climbed down from the rail and began to walk quickly through the rain, softened now to a drizzle, toward the cabin.

She had almost reached the cabin when Glenn caught up with her. "Hey, Angie, you forgot to say good night," he said, taking her by the arm.

"Good night, Glenn," she said, without looking up.

He tipped her chin up gently and forced her to look at him. In the light from the cabin, she could see the flat planes of his face shadowed by his high cheekbones. "Remember what we said tonight about Lani being able to laugh at herself?" he asked softly, holding her eyes with his. "That's what makes us human."

The raindrops beaded on Angie's lashes and ran like tears down her face. "Yes, but we weren't making fun of Lani," she said. "Not the way Shannon and her friends make fun of me. There's a big difference."

"I know," he whispered huskily. "But no matter how much it hurts, you can laugh, too. And if you can laugh at the people who try to hurt you, they'll know *you've* won." And then he kissed her, very softly and tenderly, on the lips. After a moment, he pulled back, leaving her breathless and a little shaken. "And in case nobody else has told you, Angie, you have all the symptoms of being a winner."

Angie stood by the cabin door, watching him go. In spite of the drizzle and the chilly lake breeze, she felt like turning cartwheels all around the lake.

By the next morning, the rain had stopped, and the sky was a crystalline blue. To Angie, hurrying through her early-morning shower and dashing back to the cabin with Gloria, the day seemed wonderful, full of a hundred things to look ahead to. This morning, she and Rayne were going to visit the pottery studio next to the lodge to watch a demonstration on how to make pots. After lunch, Glenn had promised her a wind-surfing lesson. This evening, of course, there was the dance. And over the promise of the whole day, like a golden sun, hung the warm memory of Glenn's good-night kiss.

"You look as if somebody just crowned you queen of Rainbow Lake," Lani said, watching Angie put on Gloria's pink lip gloss. "What happened between you and Glenn last night?"

"Oh, nothing," Angie said. She looked up and caught Lani's eye and blushed. "Well, not exactly nothing," she admitted. "I mean, he . . . he just kissed me, that's all."

Lani grinned. "He just kissed you, *that's all*? I'd say that's pretty wonderful." She turned to Rayne. "Wouldn't you?"

Rayne's eyes were puffy, and her dusky skin looked pale from lack of sleep. "Yeah," she muttered, under her breath, "wonderful."

Impulsively, Angie turned from the mirror and held out her hands, remembering how devastated Rayne had looked before she fled from thc campfire the night before. "Oh, Rayne, your singing last night was wonderful. You and Paul . . ."

"I know," Rayne interrupted bitterly. She sat on her bunk, tugging a comb through her hair. "We make beautiful music together. That's what everybody says."

"Well, you do," Gloria said. "Actually, all three of you do. You guys ought to sing together more often." She turned on the hair dryer and sat on her upper bunk, brushing her hair while she blow-dried it.

"—Until Paul decided to take off, that is," Rayne added, "without saying a word to me." She sounded angry and resentful.

"Yeah," Lani said. "We were kind of disappointed. Where'd he disappear to, anyway?"

Angie nudged Lani to get her attention and, when she looked up, shook her head warningly.

Lani stared at her with a puzzled look.

Rayne gave a bleak sigh and threw down her comb. "What Angie is trying to tell you is that Paul and I are not exactly seeing eye-to-eye these days. He left the fire because he didn't want to sing with me anymore."

"Oh, gosh. I'm sorry, Rayne," Lani said, going over to kneel in front of Rayne. She shook her head despairingly. "Is there anything I can do to help?"

Rayne ran her fingers through her long hair and leaned back on her elbows. She managed a weak smile for Lani's sake. "I know you mean well, but it's bad enough knowing Paul is angry at me without having it on tape."

Lani looked sheepish. "Well, I mean, I just thought that maybe I could talk to Paul for you, if that's what you—" She ducked the comb that Rayne threw at her.

At breakfast, Rayne and Angie sat together at a table beside a huge window overlooking the lake. The water was serene and blue, and the silvery green pines around the lodge sparkled from last night's rain. A few minutes after Angie and Rayne sat down, Ms. Richards came over, carrying a cup of coffee.

"Do you girls mind if I join you?" she asked with a smile. "I've got something to ask you."

As Angie moved her chair over, she thought how much prettier and more relaxed Ms. Richards looked than she had only two days before. Was it because of Mr. Dawson? Angie remembered that they had been together again last night, at the wiener roast. Gloria insisted that there was something going on between the two of them, and Angie had to agree now, judging from Ms. Richards's face.

Ms. Richards sat down and added a spoonful of sugar to her coffee and stirred it. "I heard you two singing last night with Paul Mitchell. You know, you sounded very good."

Rayne looked sad. "Thank you," she said, in a low voice.

"Have you been singing together long?"

Angie finished pouring milk onto her cereal and glanced up in surprise. "We've never sung together before," she said. "Last night was the first time. It sort of just happened," she explained with a laugh.

"Paul started to sing, and Rayne joined him, and then I felt like singing, too."

Ms. Richards raised her eyebrows. "I never would have guessed," she said. "You sounded as if you'd been practicing together regularly." She smiled. "Well, how would you like to sing together again—at the dance tonight? In addition to the band that will be playing, a few of the students have volunteered to perform. Margaret Prescott is going to do a stand-up comedy act, Tom Scott is going to dance, and the Carroll twins are doing one of their magic routines. Several of the seniors said last night that they would like to hear you sing again, so I thought perhaps . . ."

Rayne shook her head. "No," she said.

"But won't you even consider . . . ?"

"Please, no," Rayne said, covering her face with her hands. Her voice was muffled. "Please don't ask anymore."

Ms. Richards stared at her, puzzled. "But what . . . ?"

Angie put her hand on Ms. Richards's arm. "It would be better if we talked about it later," she said, in a low voice. "Can we have a little while to decide?"

"Take all the time you need," Ms. Richards said with a smile. She got up from the table. "I hope you decide to do it. Everyone enjoyed listening to you."

"No," Rayne said, when Ms. Richards had gone.

She pushed her plate of half-eaten pancakes away. A tear ran down the side of her nose and into the corner of her mouth. "It's all settled. And don't try to get me to change my mind, Angie. I simply *won't* sing with Paul Mitchell tonight. Not after he ran off and left me last night, sitting there all by myself looking foolish." She wiped her eyes with a paper napkin, glancing around to make sure that nobody was looking. "By now, everybody in the whole class must be gossiping about Paul and me and wondering what's wrong between us." She buried her face in her hands again. "I *hate* gossip."

"You're probably right," Angie agreed. "And they'll keep on gossiping as long as you keep on giving them something to gossip about. In fact, I suspect that lots of people know that Ms. Richards asked us to sing. If we refuse, they're bound to speculate even more about what's going on. But if all three of us stand up there together and sing, there won't be anything to gossip about, will there?" She shut her eyes. She was finally beginning to understand what Glenn had been trying to tell her last night. She could see it so clearly with Rayne, and yet for herself, it was still so hard.

Rayne sniffed. "Well . . ."

Angie opened her eyes again. "Come on, now," she countered, "what have you got to lose?"

"I know that Paul won't do it," Rayne said firmly. "He can be really stubborn sometimes. Like the way he's being about Monica."

"We won't know unless we ask him."

Rayne blew her nose into the paper napkin. "Will you"—she blew her nose again—"ask him?"

Angie shook her head. "Rayne, I've never even *met* the guy. How can I ask him?"

Rayne sighed. "All right. Will you go with me?"

Angie handed her another napkin. "Sure," she said.

They found Paul standing outside the lodge, looking forlorn and miserable. When Rayne told him about Ms. Richards's invitation, though, he brightened up a little.

He looked curiously at Angie. "You were the girl who was singing with us last night, huh? You've got a great voice. Have you done much singing before?"

Angie blushed with pleasure. "Thanks," she said. "I sang with the school chorus last year."

Rayne crossed her arms. "Well, what do you think, Paul?" she asked stiffly, as if she expected him to say no. "Should we do it?"

Paul shrugged. "I guess so," he said. "I mean, it's kind of a compliment to be asked, isn't it? That makes it sort of hard to turn down. We'll have to practice, though. Maybe this afternoon we can get together and run through a couple of songs."

Rayne looked surprised. "I...I didn't think you would want to," she said hesitantly, "after the way you went off last night."

Paul swallowed and dug the toe of his sneaker into the dirt. "Listen, Rayne, I owe you an apology for what happened last night. I mean, I'm not saying that I've changed my mind about Monica. I still think she's bad news. But it wasn't fair for me to just get up and run off the way I did. I..."

Angie turned and left, leaving the two of them alone on the path. Somehow it didn't seem like any of her business, it made her uncomfortable to hear Paul talk about Monica's reputation. It sounded a lot like what Shannon had said to Glenn.

Her thoughts were interrupted by a shout. "Hey, Angie!" It was Lani. "Are you going to the pottery demonstration?" For the first time, she wasn't carrying her tape recorder. Instead, she was wearing a Polaroid camera around her neck.

"Where's your tape recorder?" Angie asked. "Is it broken?"

Lani shook her head. "No," she said. She colored a little. "I...I just thought I would do a little in-depth research, that's all."

"In-depth?"

Lani smiled weakly. "Well, I heard Michael Summers say that he was interested in photography, and I thought that we might accidentally bump into each other. I heard that he's going to be at the pottery demonstration."

"Michael Summers?"

"That redheaded guy I was talking to last night, before you guys dragged me off and stole my tape."

"You're interested in him?"

Lani fidgeted. "Well, I don't know. But how am I ever going to recognize the perfect boyfriend if I don't have someone to compare him to? Anyway, don't you think Michael's kind of cute? Maybe a little on the skinny side, but . . ."

"Oh, sure," Angie said hastily. "Yes, I think he's really cute."

"I mean, that wasn't the only thing I liked about him," Lani said. "He was interested in talking to me about the project." She paused. "Didn't you hear?"

"Well, I really didn't get a chance to hear what he said."

"But then last night, Nancy suggested that the direct approach might not be the best way to go with everybody. So I decided that today I'd hang out where Michael was, and maybe we'll wind up talking." She pushed the hair out of her eyes. "What do you think?"

Angie put her arm around Lani. "I agree with Nancy," she said. "The direct approach *isn't* always the best way to go. I think it's a good idea to wait and see what happens." They had reached the pottery studio, which was located next to the parking lot. A group of seniors stood outside talking. Angie could see Shannon was there with some of her bunkmates. She looked great as usual in a pale yellow jump suit. Her outfit made Angie painfully aware of her old khaki shorts, marred with a big spot where she had spilled bleach on them.

"There's Michael," Lani whispered urgently. "He looks even cuter today." She squared her shoulders and started to walk away. "Well, wish me luck," she said.

As Lani walked away, Angie heard the loud roar of a car, revving noisily through the parking lot. It sounded awfully familiar. No! It couldn't be! The car screeched to a stop beside her with a sudden squeal of rubber, and the driver leaned out the window.

"Hey, kid! How'ya doin'?"

It was Tony.

Chapter Eleven

"What exactly are we looking for?" Nancy asked, as Gloria parked the Belvederes' Mazda in the Forest Glen Mall parking lot. The Belvederes were spending the weekend at the beach house in Half Moon Bay, and Mrs. Daniels had gone to visit her grandchildren, but Gloria was sure that nobody would mind if she borrowed the car. After all, she used it frequently to run errands, and she knew where the key was kept.

Gloria considered Nancy's question. "We're looking for a *spectacular* dress," she said, "a designer dress that looks like it cost a million bucks." With a sharp pang, she thought about the slender balance in her checking account. The money she had earned this summer was supposed to go toward her college fund. But the dress was more important right now, wasn't it?

Nancy looked at her as they climbed out of the car and began to walk toward the mall. "Let's see if I've got this right," she said. "You want a dress that *looks like* it cost a lot of money. Right?"

Gloria nodded, thinking about Mademoiselle, the small exclusive dress shop she had visited once with Mrs. Belvedere. That's where they would start looking. "Yes," she said, "something that's really unique —something classic."

"You want this dress so you can impress Tim. Right?" Nancy pursued.

"Yes, that's right," Gloria said, glancing at her friend with a puzzled frown. "I mean, is there anything wrong with that? Don't you buy clothes to impress people sometimes?"

"—So you can impress Tim with how much money you have to spend on a dress. Right?"

Gloria swiveled to face Nancy, feeling both hurt and impatient. Her best friend, of all people, should understand. "Nancy, did you come with me to help me buy a new dress, or did you come to give me a lecture on why I *shouldn't* buy a new dress?"

Nancy bit her lip and looked away. "Well, neither one, exactly."

"Well, what do you mean, *exactly*?" Gloria asked,

as they entered the mall. It was early, so there weren't too many people around, and their footsteps echoed in the half-empty corridor.

"I came with you," Nancy said, hurrying to keep up with Gloria, "to tell you that I think you ought to stop deceiving Tim about who you really are."

"Do we have to talk about this stuff again today?" Gloria pleaded. "I thought we'd been all through it yesterday and the day before."

"Yeah, we've been through it before," Nancy conceded. "But I've thought about it some more, and I don't see how any relationship can survive if the people involved aren't totally honest with each other. If Sam had been honest with me, I could have avoided a lot of pain. You're not being honest with Tim."

"Do you think I *like* the way things are?" Gloria asked miserably. They stopped in front of Mademoiselle, and Gloria stared into its display window, full of artfully arranged mannequins wearing incredibly expensive dresses and suits. "Do you think I really *enjoy* the suspense of wondering if Tim is going to find out accidentally that I'm not who he thinks I am?"

With a clutch of sadness, Gloria remembered what Tim had said the night before about the fun they would have together next year. It was obvious that he thought the two of them would fit, easily and naturally, into his parents' social scene, where women wore dresses and suits exactly like the ones in the window in front of her. But *she* couldn't fit into that kind of world, the world of dinner parties, and theater, and leisurely weekends at a private resort. That wasn't *her* world. Her world was full of ordinary things, like trying not to be late for school because her parents' secondhand car wouldn't start again and baby-sitting for money to buy clothes and worrying about whether she had enough left over for a pizza on Friday night after the football game. When Tim found out what her world was *really* like, his feelings for her were bound to change. She would lose him. She knew it. And the thought sliced her insides like a jagged knife.

"Well, maybe you don't *enjoy* the suspense," Nancy pointed out, "but you're certainly not doing anything to change it. You've had a half dozen chances to tell him, but every time you think of another excuse."

Gloria leaned her forehead against the cool glass and stared at a mannequin in a beautiful red dress, posed languidly on a wrought-iron bench, its wrists and throat laden with glittering jewelry. At that moment, Gloria would have given anything to change places with it and have nothing to do and nothing to think about.

"I *can't* change it," Gloria said, in a low voice. "Not today, anyway. Not tonight." She turned away from the window to face Nancy. "Don't you understand?" she cried miserably. "After tonight, everything is going to turn back into pumpkins and mice. All I want is just one night to remember—just one magic, fairy-tale night, where I'm the beautiful, glamorous princess that Tim thinks I am. After that, I'll be content to go back to being a scullery maid." She swallowed. "I'm going to tell him tomorrow. I've already decided."

"Really?" Nancy asked hopefully. "Really, truly? You're not just saying that?"

"Yes, really, truly," Gloria said, resigned. "I'm going to tell him tomorrow."

Nancy reached for her hand. "Well, if you honestly mean that, I guess I don't have anything left to say except good luck."

For a minute, Gloria stared down at their joined hands. "If we've said everything there is to be said, can we go buy a dress?" she asked finally. Somehow it didn't feel like as much fun as it had a little while before.

After trying on a dozen dresses, Gloria finally decided on a sapphire-blue chiffon with a full skirt that swished around her legs and made her *feel* like a princess. It was on sale for half price, so she didn't even have to empty her checking account to pay for it. Carrying the dress, carefully boxed, the two girls made their way through the parking lot to the car.

Gloria unlocked the door. "Well, now that we have the dress, I have to think about the rest of my outfit," she said, getting in and leaning over to open Nancy's door. "I've got a pair of shoes that will be perfect, so that's no problem. But jewelry—that's something else."

"How about the string of pearls that you got for Christmas last year?" Nancy asked, putting the dress box into the backseat. "They would look pretty against that blue."

Gloria put the key into the ignition, shaking her head. "They're nice, but they look exactly like what they are—fake pearls. Anybody who could afford a dress like the one I just bought could also afford *real* pearls."

And then Gloria thought of the perfect complement to the dress: Mrs. Belvedere's sapphire pendant. It was exactly the same color. The only problem, of course, was that Mrs. Belvedere was gone, and she couldn't ask permission to borrow it. She would have to think of something else.

"Well, let's see," Nancy said, settling into the seat and rolling down the window, "there's my grandmother's diamond pin, but it's at home. And anyway, I'm not sure my mother would let us have it. She's kind of sentimental about it."

Gloria laughed. "Sounds like a long shot to me." She turned on the ignition and drove out of the lot, glancing over her shoulder to check for cars. She found that she couldn't push the thought of the pendant out of her mind. It *was* the perfect complement to her new dress. In fact, the more she thought about it, the more it seemed as if the dress would be incomplete *without* the pendant.

She drove down the highway in silence, thinking. Well, maybe she should just go ahead and borrow it anyway. She borrowed lots of things from the Belvederes, and they never seemed to mind. In fact, they always encouraged her to use whatever she needed —like the car, for instance. Of course, they were usually there to say yes when she asked. But Mrs. Belvedere wouldn't have to know a thing about it, since she was away until Sunday night. The pendant would be back in its box early Sunday morning. It would be easy.

It might be easy, but it isn't *right,* a tiny voice inside her said. It isn't yours. Borrowing it without asking is just the same as *stealing* it. Gloria shivered guiltily, but she made up her mind to borrow the pendant anyway. She could just imagine how it would sparkle against her throat, how it would impress Tim. She felt certain Mrs. Belvedere wouldn't mind, at least, that's what she kept telling herself.

"It's okay, Nancy," she said slowly. "I've already decided about the jewelry."

"Oh?" Nancy asked curiously. "What is it?"

"Oh, just . . . just a piece of costume jewelry," Gloria said, feeling horribly sneaky. She couldn't tell Nancy what she was going to do. And that made her feel even worse.

When they got to the Belvederes', Gloria parked the car in the garage, and the two of them went into the empty house.

"Wow!" Nancy gulped, looking around at the sumptuous, high-ceilinged rooms tastefully decorated with elegant furnishings. "You've been living *here* all summer? No wonder you have delusions of grandeur!" She paused reverently in front of a gigantic red-and-blue painting that took up most of the dining room wall. "Wow! Is this an *original* Matisse?"

Gloria laughed. "It is, and there's another one in the foyer. The Belvederes collect art the way you and I collect postcards. Wait here a minute. I just have to get a few things from upstairs."

When Gloria got to Mrs. Belvedere's room, she switched on the light and went over to the vanity. To her relief, the jewelry box was there. She opened it and found the pendant in its special place. She picked it up and held it to the light. At the center was a large, multifaceted sapphire, surrounded by a circlet of sparkling diamonds. The pendant was suspended from a delicate gold chain. It's perfect, she thought, exactly the color of my new dress. Gloria suppressed a pang of guilt as she slipped the pendant into her purse and left the room. Something deep inside her told her that what she was doing was wrong, taking an awfully big risk. But it felt to her as if everything she had done lately was a risk. She would return the pendant in the morning, and no one would be the wiser. She joined Nancy in the living room and glanced at her watch. "Hey, you know what?" she said. "If we hurry, we can get to the lodge in time for lunch."

Gloria and Nancy were crossing the parking lot after dropping off the new dress in the cabin when Nancy suddenly stopped. She pointed to a red GTO with streamers of flame running along both sides and a dragon painted on the hood. "You know, I think that's the car that Angie came in the other day. The one she had to climb out the window of."

"Whose car is it?" Gloria asked.

"I guess it belongs to her brother. I think his name is Tony. You know, the guy who's out on probation for shoplifting, or something. I wonder what *he's* doing here?"

The two girls hurried to the lodge. In the dining room, they filled their plates at the salad bar and looked around. In a distant corner, far away from everybody else, Angie was sitting with a swarthy, muscular boy in a black T-shirt with the sleeves cut off. She had her back to everybody, but it was clear from her hunched shoulders and bowed head that she was miserable.

Gloria and Nancy exchanged looks. "Maybe we shouldn't butt in," Nancy said hesitantly. "Let's eat with Lani and Rayne."

Gloria shook her head. "No, I think we ought to go sit with Angie and her brother," she said. "Look at Angie. You can tell how awful she feels, just from the way she's sitting."

"It looks like they want to be alone," Nancy observed.

"Maybe not," Gloria objected. "I think Angie's just hiding over there because she's embarrassed. Come on, I really think we should go keep her company. You know how much she worries about what people think of her family. If we ignore her now, she'll think we're not her friends."

Nancy shifted her tray uneasily. "Well, I . . ."

"Come on," Gloria urged again. "Tell you what.

Let's go get Rayne and Lani, and we'll *all* go sit with them."

It took a little bit of convincing, but in the end, Lani and Rayne agreed. They made quite a parade, trooping across the dining room. Gloria hoped that everybody was looking at them. When they got to Angie's table, she looked up, surprised.

Gloria held out her hand. "Tony, I'm Gloria Larsen, one of Angie's bunkmates."

Tony flushed and pushed back his chair. "Pleased to meet you," he muttered, standing up. After all the girls had introduced themselves, they sat down.

Gloria opened her milk. "Well, what do you think of Rainbow Lake?" she asked Tony.

Tony fidgeted uneasily. "It's . . . it's kinda nice," he said. "I mean, I haven't seen much of it, but . . ."

"Tony just got here," Angie broke in hurriedly. "Just before the pottery demonstration. We went down to look at the beach for a few minutes, but then it was time for lunch."

"Well, we're glad you came," Nancy said. She looked as if she didn't quite mean it, Gloria thought, but maybe Tony wouldn't notice.

He looked surprised. "Yeah? Well, I just figured I'd like a little drive in the country," he said shrugging. "You know, with work and all, there's not much time to get out of the city." He grinned at Angie. "And

Angie here talked so much about the good time she was gonna have with all her fancy friends this weekend. I just figured I'd like to meet some of 'em."

Angie flushed. "I didn't say anything about 'fancy' friends, Tony," she protested.

Tony laughed. "Sorry, kid. Sometimes I get carried away. You know how I am." He looked at the group around the table. "Your friends, huh? Looks like you ain't doin' too bad for yourself."

Gloria put her hand on Angie's arm. "Listen, I wouldn't know what to do without Angie. She's a whiz when it comes to knowing exactly the right moment to dump potato salad on people."

"And she knows all the words to 'Puff the Magic Dragon,' too," Rayne added.

"And she's an expert when it comes to beach-front robbery," Lani chimed in.

Tony looked confused. "Sounds like you've been having a great time," he said. He pushed back his chair and stood up. "Well, I gotta get goin'. I promised the boss I'd work the late shift tonight."

Gloria nudged Nancy, and they got up too. "We'll walk you out to the parking lot," she said. "Come on, everybody."

"But I'm not through eating," Lani objected, her sandwich halfway to her mouth.

Gloria kicked her surreptitiously. "Come on,

Lani," she said. "It'll still be here when you get back."

As they followed Angie and Tony out the door, Gloria could feel the eyes of everyone in the dining room on them. For a moment, it almost seemed as if Angie's embarrassment might prove contagious. But Gloria's self-consciousness didn't last. Let them think what they want, she told herself staunchly. Tony isn't really such a bad guy, and the important thing is, we didn't let Angie down.

Chapter Twelve

The five of them stood watching Tony race out of the parking lot, leaving a dark rubber streak on the pavement and a cloud of exhaust in the air behind him. "He certainly drives *fast*, doesn't he," Nancy said weakly, as the red GTO screeched around the corner on two wheels and disappeared around the curve.

Angie looked over at Nancy, but the tears in her eyes made it hard for her to see. Everything was a blur. She felt ripped into a hundred little pieces inside—as if her whole world had exploded into fragments. From the minute Tony had arrived, Angie had felt like crawling into a hole in the ground. Shannon and her friends had stood around whispering and pointing at her. Angie was sure she knew exactly what they were saying.

"It's him, Angie Maroni's criminal brother. Well, birds of a feather flock together, they always say. And don't forget what her father did, too. Like father, like daughter. You'll never be able to trust people like that. Hang on to your money, everybody."

As quickly as she could, Angie had gotten Tony away from the group, away from their taunts and pointing fingers. The two of them had gone down to the beach, and she had made sure they stayed there until it was time for lunch. But lunch had been even worse—they shouldn't have gone to the dining room, where everybody could stare at them and gossip. By that time, all the seniors knew that Tony had arrived. Everybody knew who he was—and what he was. Shannon Welles and her friends made sure of that.

Despairingly, Angie shook her head. She should have asked Tony to wait while she packed her things and then ridden home with him. Why hadn't she? There was no point in sticking around for the wind-surfing lesson with Glenn or the dance tonight. After all, she *was* a Maroni. She was completely out of place here with all these people, including her bunk-mates. No matter how much they pretended to like her, they were like all the rest.

"You didn't have to come and rescue me," she blurted out, over the lump in her throat. Her voice came out all cracked and funny sounding. "I mean, I was perfectly happy sitting there talking to my brother all by myself. I was doing okay."

"You were?" Gloria tucked her arm into Angie's and began to walk with her in the direction of the lodge. The others came along close behind. "Gee, that's strange. Then I guess we ought to give you the Oscar for best actress of the year. The rest of us could have sworn that you were definitely *not* okay. In fact, you looked pretty miserable, sitting over there in the corner, just the two of you. From where we stood, it looked like what you needed was a few friends to come and cheer you up."

"Well, you were wrong," Angie began defensively. "I didn't need any cheering..." Then she hiccuped. She always hiccuped when she was trying not to cry.

"Get a paper bag and breathe into it," Nancy offered helpfully. "I read that carbon monoxide is sometimes good for hiccups."

"That's carbon *dioxide*," Lani corrected with a laugh.

"Well, I've heard that the best cure for hiccups is to finish the lunch that you didn't finish ten minutes ago," Gloria put in.

"Oh, my gosh, that's right!" Lani exclaimed. "I left half a sandwich just sitting there, alone and unprotected. I hope nobody has cleared the table."

"I think Gloria's right," Rayne said. "In fact," she added, clapping her hand over her mouth, "I have this horrible feeling that I'm going to get the hiccups too if I don't finish my salad."

"Right," Nancy agreed. "And I sort of feel that having a double dip of chocolate ice cream will keep me from ever getting the hiccups again."

Gloria put her arm around Angie's shoulders. "We've taken a poll of the Filthy Five," she said. "The vote is four to nothing that finishing lunch is the best cure for hiccups."

Angie shook her head again. What had she ever done to deserve such friends? "Make that five to nothing," she said in a small voice, and she hiccuped again.

After lunch, everybody went back to the cabin to get changed. Angie stripped off her jeans and tugged on her old blue swimsuit, worrying a little about what looked like a run in the back. She thought of Glenn's promise to give her a wind-surfing lesson that afternoon. Angie was sure that he had seen Tony this morning—and if he hadn't, Shannon would have told him all about it by now. After that episode, he probably wouldn't want to have anything to do with her. She sighed and combed her hair and put on a touch of the pink lip gloss that she and Gloria were sharing. Well, maybe it would be better if Glenn didn't even show up. Then at least she would know where she stood with him.

But he did show up. When she got down to the beach, he was already there, wearing his swimsuit and a crumpled white canvas beach hat, standing beside what looked like a surfboard with a big red-and-white sail. The sky was blue and cloudless, and a breeze blew out of the south, ruffling the surface of the water in little cats-paw ripples.

"Hi," he said. "All set for a sailing lesson?" He grinned at her, but Angie thought that there was something else in his eyes, something she hadn't seen before. He seemed . . . well, somehow he seemed a little nervous, perhaps even edgy. Was he worrying about his reputation?

"Sure," Angie said. She waited for him to say something else, maybe something about Tony's appearance in the dining room at lunch, but he didn't.

"Well, then," he said, in a businesslike tone, "let me show you how this thing works before we take it out in the water. Have you ever been in a small sailboat?"

Angie shook her head.

"Well, it's not important. A wind surfer works sort of like a little boat, except there's no tiller. Instead, you steer it by moving the sail and your body. You make it move forward, into the wind, by counterbalancing the weight of your body against the weight of the wind that strikes the sail. See?" He stood on the board and demonstrated. "You just point the board and the sail into the wind, lean back, and balance yourself. You have to use your knees a lot. In that way, it's like skiing." He threw her a hopeful look. "Have you ever been skiing?"

Angie shook her head again, a cold knot forming at the pit of her stomach. "No, I've never been skiing," she said in a low voice.

"Well, okay, then," Glenn said with a lopsided smile, "Let's just take it out on the lake, and I'll show you how to do it. Then you can try it for yourself and see what happens."

"Hold it!"

Angie turned. It was Lani, looking through her Polaroid camera at them. Suddenly conscious of her old blue swimsuit, Angie stepped quickly behind the sail.

"What did you do that for, Angie?" Lani complained. "I got a good picture of Glenn, but now I'll have to get another one of you."

"Later," Glenn told her. "Angie and I have a date with the lake just now." With a deft move, he took the sail down, and together they paddled the wind surfer out into deep water, leaving Lani waving at them from the beach. Glenn clambered up on the water-slick board and pulled the sail up, holding on to the bar across the middle of the sail. "All you have to do is to hang on to this bar," he shouted as he criss-crossed the waves in front of Angie. "Use the weight of your body to get leverage against the weight of the sail, and let the wind pull you through the water." He dumped the wind surfer, splashing into the water beside her. "Okay, now it's your turn, Angie." He righted the board. "Just climb on, reach over and grab the bar, and pull the sail up toward you."

Shivering, Angie tried to climb on, but the board was slippery, and she immediately tipped over and slid off into the water with a splash. The second time, the sail came loose, and Glenn had to put it back again. Finally, with a boost from Glenn, she managed to scramble up on the board, grab the bar, and lift the sail awkwardly toward her.

"Great!" Glenn shouted, treading water beside her. "Now just point into the wind and hang on!"

"The wind?" Angie cried, struggling for balance on the wobbly board. "Which way . . . ?" Just then a strong puff of wind hit the sail, and before she knew it she was back in the water again.

"I'm sorry," Glenn said contritely. "I guess I left something out. Actually, it helps if you check to see which direction the wind is blowing from and get the board pointed into the wind *before* you get on. Today, we've got a southern breeze. So let's turn the board that way."

On her second try, Angie managed to mount the board, lift the sail smoothly, and take off. The feeling of lift and power was exhilarating, and instinctively she leaned backward, holding on to the bar and balancing her weight against the thrust of the wind in the sail.

"Terrific!" Glenn called, swimming along behind her. "Now you've got the hang of it! But don't lean too—"

Splash! This time, the wind-surfer sail came over on top of Angie, and she disappeared under a billow of wet Dacron.

"Are you okay?" Glenn asked, paddling over to her.

Angie swam out from under the sail and brushed the water out of her eyes. "Yeah, I'm okay," she said disgustedly, trying to cough the water out of her lungs. "But I can't understand how anybody ever *learns* how to wind surf! You can't stay balanced on it long enough to learn how to stay balanced on it!" Coughing hard, she clung to the board. "I feel so clumsy."

"You're not clumsy," Glenn said comfortingly. "You're just inexperienced. You can't expect to be an expert the first couple of times you try." He put his hand on her arm. His fingers were warm against her chilly flesh. "As a matter of fact, I think you're doing pretty well. You've got the idea of what it takes to balance the board, now all you need is practice—and to not mind falling off every thirty seconds or so for the first hour." He laughed. "During the summer I teach Red Cross swimming classes, and you should see some of the kids trying to keep their heads above water. Ever try to teach a rock to swim? It's a real challenge, believe me!"

Angie had to laugh at that, even though laughing made her start coughing again.

"Hey, Glenn!" There was a loud hail from nearby, and another wind surfer zipped up behind them. It was Shannon, her ash-blond hair flowing in the wind. To Angie, she looked incredibly sexy in an electric blue bikini and amazingly expert as she maneuvered the board across the waves. She stalled it just as she reached them. "It's time for the races. Are you ready to go?"

Glenn glanced at Angie. "Well, right now I . . ."

"Craig has been counting on you to help with this," Shannon beguiled. She darted a quick, scornful glance at Angie. "Hey, Angie, how did your brother enjoy his visit to Rainbow Lake?"

Angie started to speak, but Shannon went on, turning her attention back to Glenn, "Now, don't back out on us, Glenn. You promised Craig that you'd help with the scoring, too. Remember?"

"Yeah." Glenn nodded. He colored a little. "Yeah, I remember." He turned to Angie and brushed the shock of wet hair out of his eyes. "What you need more than anything else, Angie, is lots of practice. Would you mind if I . . . ? I mean, I really did promise Craig that I would help him with the races. I thought he was going to start an hour or two later, but if they're ready to go now, I . . ."

"It's okay, Glenn," Angie said, trying not to sound disappointed. "I understand."

"Thanks, Angie," Glenn said gratefully. "I realize I . . ." There was that odd look in his eyes again. Angie couldn't figure it out. "Listen, about tonight . . ."

"Are you coming, Glenn?" Shannon interrupted impatiently. "Hop on behind me, and let's go."

The board lumbered away slowly toward the beach under the weight of the two of them. Angie floated in the water for a few minutes longer, clinging to the bobbing wind surfer. What had Glenn meant about tonight? Well, there was no way to know now—he had already picked up another board on the beach, and he and Shannon were racing across the waves, like two sea gulls skimming together across the surface of the lake. Angie could hear Shannon's silvery laughter shimmering over the water.

She spent the next hour alone, trying clumsily to master the intricacies of the wind surfer. By the end of it, she was completely worn out with the effort of climbing onto the board and holding it into the wind. She had finally managed to work her way back to the beach, where she collapsed, soggy and exhausted, on the warm sand.

After a few minutes of rest, she sat up. Not very far offshore, she could see a cluster of red, yellow, and blue sails rounding an orange buoy. It was Glenn and Shannon and their friends, riding free and easy across the waves, enjoying the afternoon's race. She looked down at her hands. Her palms were blistery red, her fingers sore from gripping the sail bar, and her toes pocked and wrinkled like prunes from spending nearly two hours in the water. Her arms were weary from the unaccustomed strain of maneuvering the sail, her knees were sore from the constant shifting, and her shoulders and face felt sunburned. She twisted to look over her shoulder. And yes, there was the run in her swimsuit, just as she had feared. Had it been there when Glenn was watching her fall off the board like a clumsy kid? She laughed bitterly to herself. Teach a rock to swim? He must be telling everybody how challenging it was to teach a rock to *sail*. She looked back out over the lake again, shading her eyes with her hand. Let the rest of them play their stupid sailing games. She was going back to the cabin to take a nap.

Chapter Thirteen

"Where's Angie?" Gloria asked, coming into the cabin and tossing her wet towel onto the bunk. She had spent the afternoon playing volleyball with the girls in the next cabin and had just come back from taking a shower.

Lani looked up from her notebook. "You just missed her. She and Rayne went over to the lodge to practice with Paul. Did you know they're singing tonight?"

Gloria nodded. "Rayne told me this morning at breakfast." She climbed up into the upper bunk and lay down on her stomach, resting her chin on her hands. "How did Angie's wind-surfing lesson with Glenn turn out?"

Lani put down her pen and looked troubled. "Well,

she didn't say. She just came in and flopped down on her bunk and fell sound asleep. She had sand all over her, and she was sunburned. When Rayne woke her up to go practice, she got dressed without saying a word. She looked a little groggy. Maybe she was still sleepy—or waterlogged. Or maybe she's still upset about Tony's visit this morning. Why do you suppose he came?" Lani giggled. "To case the joint?" Then she immediately looked ashamed at what she had said. "I didn't mean that," she corrected herself hastily. "Bad joke. Tacky."

Gloria shook her head. Poor Angie. Sometimes her own problems seemed almost overwhelming, but when she compared them to Angie's, they didn't seem so terrible. "It doesn't sound too good," she agreed. "If things had gone okay with Glenn, I'm sure she would have been really cheerful and excited about it."

Lani fished in her camera bag. "I tried to get a picture of her and Glenn when they were out on the beach, but she ducked behind the sail. All I got was Glenn." She came across to Gloria's bunk and handed Gloria the picture of Glenn in his swimsuit and white beach hat, squinting narrow eyed into the sun.

Gloria stared at it. "He really *is* cute, isn't he?" She handed the picture back to Lani with a little shake of her head. "Do you think Angie has a chance with him?"

"I don't have any idea. I'm the one who has no experience with things like this, remember?" Lani replied with a sigh. She took the picture and put it on her shelf. "What do you think?"

"Angie's got a lot going for her, if she would only wake up and realize it," Gloria said. "Her problem is that she just can't seem to get over this ridiculous idea that everybody is better than she is. Just because—"

The door crashed open. "Stupid jerk!" Nancy flung herself into the room and threw herself on her bunk. "Why do boys have to be so . . . so totally weird! They're absolutely unbelievable!" She yanked the pillow over her head and turned her face to the wall.

From her perch in the upper bunk, Gloria peered down at Nancy. "My goodness," she said wonderingly, hanging upside down over the edge of the bed. "What's eating you?"

Nancy jerked the pillow off and rolled over to glare at Gloria. "Nothing's eating me," she snapped and put the pillow over her face again.

"Well, par-don me," Gloria said. "I could have sworn that something nasty was nibbling away at you and giving you a slight pain. But I could be wrong," she went on.

Nancy got up and went to the mirror to comb her

hair. "Well, if you have to know, I just found out that Sam called me." She picked up the picture of Glenn, looked at it, and put it back. She began to pace up and down the room.

"Sam?" Lani scratched her head. "Who's Sam?"

"Sam is this guy that Nancy met in San Diego," Gloria told her. "The one who forgot to tell her about his steady girl friend." She turned back to Nancy. "What did he want?"

"I don't have the slightest idea," Nancy said, still pacing. "That's the worst of it. I mean, I called home just now, the way I promised my mother I would. And she told me that Sam called last night." She moaned and sat back down on the edge of the bunk and covered her face with her hands. "Oh, God, I don't *need* this. Boys are so *stupid*."

Gloria got down and went over and put her arms around Nancy. "Nobody *needs* it," she said, thinking about Tim. "But most of the time there isn't anything we can do about boys. We just have to learn to cope with them, that's all."

At that moment Rayne came into the cabin, followed by Angie. Rayne looked more cheerful than she had all weekend, but Angie had a sad, wistful look on her face. "Does either of you have some useful suggestions on coping with boys?" Nancy asked.

"I don't know about suggestions," Lani said, "but

I do have one simple observation."

"What's that?" Gloria asked suspiciously. She was learning that when Lani made a suggestion, you'd better watch out.

"From all my research so far," Lani said, "I have observed that whenever a girl and a boy become involved, there is only one outcome—total confusion and utter misunderstanding. Chaos. It seems to be inevitable." A sudden look of enthusiasm came into her eyes, and she sat up straighter. "You know, Gloria, maybe what we need is a workshop on boy-girl communications, where we could get all this stuff out into the open and learn how to talk to one another. As a matter of fact, I would be glad to organize . . ."

The girls all looked at one another. "Lani Connors, this time you've gone too far!" Gloria said. All together, she and Angie and Rayne and Nancy descended on Lani and dragged her, kicking and screaming and laughing, into the middle of the room and began to hit her with Nancy's pillows.

"Gloria, you look stunning!" Lani said in a hushed voice, as Gloria turned around in front of her, the full skirt whirling into a wide circle. "That dress is a dream! And your necklace—the color is a perfect match. It's as though the two were made for each other!"

"Is that the necklace you borrowed from Mrs. Belvedere?" Nancy asked. "It looks expensive. Are you sure she said it was okay?"

"Yes," Gloria fibbed, a wave of guilt washing over her. She stared at herself in the mirror. The dress was exactly the right color for her, and the diamonds surrounding the sapphire sparkled brightly against the blue chiffon. The pendant was the perfect touch. If only she didn't feel so guilty about borrowing it without permission. No matter how many times she'd tried to rationalize that she wasn't *stealing*, she still felt like a dirty sneak. What if Mrs. Belvedere came home unexpectedly and found the pendant missing? What if...?

Gloria shook herself and pushed the troublesome thoughts away. The pendant *looked* so right, surely it had to *be* all right that she had borrowed it, too. As Lani had said, it looked exactly as if it were made to go with the dress. It was as if fate were pointing the way for her to wear it.

She turned to Nancy. "Well, I guess my fairy godmother did a pretty good job." She laughed as lightly as she could. "Now if only the mice and the pumpkins manage to hold out until midnight..." She began to search on the shelf beside her bed for her lip gloss. "Say, have you seen my new pink lip gloss anywhere?"

"Angie's been using it," Lani said, pulling on her panty hose. "Maybe she took it with her. She and Rayne left in a hurry."

Gloria frowned. "I don't know why she'd take it. We were sharing it, but she knew I needed it, too."

"Here"—Nancy pawed through her purse—"I've got some that's almost the same shade. Use this."

Gloria tried it on. "Actually, I like this even better," she said.

"You can keep it," Nancy said generously. "I have some I'd rather use."

There was a tentative knock at the door, and Gloria went to open it. Tim was standing outside, looking strangely formal and very handsome in a dark suit and tie, his still-damp hair combed back. She could smell the spicy scent of after-shave. When he saw her, his eyes widened, and he took a deep breath. "Wow," he said, nearly inaudibly.

Gloria giggled. "Is that all you can say?" she asked gaily.

For a few seconds Tim just stood there. "No," he said at last. "But you'll have to give me a minute to catch my breath and collect my thoughts. I've only seen you in blue jeans or a swimsuit all summer. You've sort of . . . taken me by surprise."

"What I should have said," Tim said, when they were sitting down at their table on the lodge deck, "is that you look very beautiful"—he reached across the white cloth for her hand—"absolutely beautiful. Your dress, your pendant . . ." He leaned forward and touched the pendant, and Gloria shivered. "You know, you have terrific taste, Gloria. You know how to choose *exactly* the right thing.

Gloria blushed. "Thank you," she murmured, wondering if Cinderella had felt like this when Prince Charming chose her from among all the other princesses. And how did Prince Charming feel when he discovered that his elegant princess had gone back to sweep out her kitchen after the ball?

Tim leaned back and looked out over the lake. The last rosy blush of sunset stained the western sky, and the stars were pinpoint diamonds. The air, fragrant with crisp pine, had just a hint of autumn chill. "You know, I've been thinking about the last few weeks here," he said lazily. "It's been so perfect, I wish it didn't have to end. But I'm so glad I met you this summer, and the other kids from Glenwood. Now it won't be so strange to start my senior year at a new school."

He picked up his glass of iced tea. "Here's to Glenwood, and to our senior year—and to us."

Gloria picked up her glass and touched the rim to

his. "To our senior year," she replied.

"And to us," Tim repeated, with a warm, caressing look.

"To us," she said slowly.

Ginger had outdone herself with the dinner. Everyone agreed that it had been perfect—the food, the service, the table decorations. Afterwards, the tables were cleared away, and everyone gathered in the main room of the lodge where the dance was going to be held. But first it was time for the student performances.

Gloria and Tim sat together on the floor near the fireplace with Lani. At the front of the room, Ms. Richards, with her hair pinned up elegantly and wearing a white dress that showed off her tan, went up to the small stage to introduce the acts.

"One of the traditions of Senior Orientation Weekend," she said, "is a talent showcase. We've asked several of our seniors to give us a preview of some of the things we have to look forward to during the year. We've got four fine acts for you, beginning with Margaret Prescott, who's going to do one of her famous comedy routines."

Margaret, a short, plump blond girl with a wry sense of humor, was used to entertaining at parties in Glenwood. Her jokes and off-the-wall humor did a great job of loosening everybody up with laughter. After Margaret finished her act, Tom Scott came on with an old soft-shoe burlesque number and some stunning acrobatics. Then the Carrol twins, Mark and Matthew, dressed in dark suits, long capes, and tall black hats, did a half dozen magic tricks, starting with the familiar rabbit-in-the-hat trick. Only this time, they didn't use a hat. They used one of Ginger's big salad bowls, with the lettuce still in it.

"Now, for our next trick," Mark announced in a deep voice, "we need a volunteer from the audience." He looked around. "Gloria, how about you?" he asked, pointing to Gloria. "Will you volunteer?"

"Me?" she asked. She shook her head. "No, please," she said, "I don't want to."

"Oh, go on," Tim whispered, grinning. "It's just a little magic. Go ahead." He gave her a playful shove.

Gloria stood up and went to the front, feeling foolish and wondering why she had been chosen. In a way, she was glad. Now everyone would have a chance to see her new dress.

Mark winked at her when she got to the stage. "Hello, beautiful," he said. He put his arm around her and sniffed her perfume. "My, you smell good," he said loudly.

Gloria giggled with embarrassment. Everybody laughed.

"Actually, it isn't you I'm interested in at all," Mark went on, staring pointedly at Gloria's pendant. "It's that piece of jewelry you're wearing. It's stunning. In fact, it's exactly what I've always wanted."

Gloria felt her heart stop. Was she going to have to take the pendant off? What was he going to do with it? She wished she had listened to her instincts and refused to be part of the act.

"Now, don't worry about a thing, Gloria," Mark said soothingly, patting her on the arm. "I've never lost a stage prop yet—not on purpose, anyway." Everybody laughed again.

With trembling fingers, Gloria unfastened the pendant. "Please be careful," she whispered, handing it to him. Her fingers felt stiff and icy.

"Now, if you'll watch me," Mark intoned, in a stage-magician's voice, "I will show you . . ." He opened his hand. The pendant was gone. "Oh, no," he growled, "I must have mislaid it already." He fished unsuccessfully in his pockets and then came over to Gloria. "Oh, here it is," he said, putting his hand up to her ear and pulling the pendant out. He gave her a mock glare. "I thought you said you were a *volunteer*," he said. "I'd call you an Indian giver." The audience howled.

He went back to the center of the stage, where Matthew joined him. "Now, we want to show you . . ."

For the next five minutes, Gloria stood off to the side, watching the pendant appear in Mark's hands and then reappear in Matthew's, flying from one pocket to another, from one box to another, into one hat and out another. She held her breath the whole time until the pendant was back safely around her neck. What if it had gotten broken somehow? she thought, as she made her way back to her place beside Tim. What if one of the diamonds had come loose? Why in the world had she borrowed it in the first place? It had been a crazy thing to do.

After the Carrol twins, Angie, Rayne, and Paul came on to do "Puff the Magic Dragon" again and two love songs. They sang very simply, with only Paul's guitar as accompaniment. The quiet harmony of their voices held everyone spellbound. Rayne and Paul sang without taking their eyes off each other, and Gloria couldn't help hoping that they had settled the differences that had made Rayne so unhappy. But of the three, Gloria thought that Angie's voice was the most beautiful. She sang in a husky alto that seemed to express a world of deeply felt but restrained emotion. When the singing was over, everyone applauded wildly. Glenn was seated next to Shannon, just in front of Gloria and Tim, and Gloria saw that he clapped loudest of all. Shannon didn't even bother to pretend that she was clapping.

The dance began after the talent presentations were over. One of the boys had agreed to serve as DJ for the evening. The lights were turned low, and there was a flickering fire in the stone fireplace. When the music began, a slow, sensuous song, Tim held out his arms to Gloria. "Dance?" he asked.

Gloria floated into his arms. It was the first time they had danced together, but she felt as if they had been dancing together all their lives. They followed each other perfectly, and Tim's arms around her felt warm and secure. With her cheek against his shoulder, she could almost imagine that this wonderful, magic-filled night would go on forever.

After they had danced for a while, they went into the game room and played Ping-Pong, laughing uproariously when Fluffy, the lodge cat, decided to join in the game. Then they went into the dining room, where Max Howard was sitting at the grand piano. Rayne and Paul and Angie and several others were there, and an impromptu sing-along was under way. Impulsively, Gloria went to the piano, too. They were singing some old songs from the thirties, and the next thing she knew, she found herself seated on the piano, doing a throaty Marlene Dietrich imitation, Tim urging her on. With Tim, Gloria was beginning to discover, she felt so easy and free that she was willing to do things she had been too timid to do before, like volunteering for the magic tricks, and singing from atop the piano. It must be part of the wonder of the evening, she decided happily, as they went out on the dance floor again and she melted into Tim's arms.

A little later, Gloria went into the rest room to freshen up her makeup. Nancy was there, changing out of the black uniform she had worn to help Ginger serve dinner and putting on a dress.

"I'm almost too tired to dance," Nancy said, yawning. "Maybe I should just go back to the cabin and get some sleep."

"Well, I told you to stay out of the kitchen," Gloria teased, looking in the mirror as she applied the lip gloss she had borrowed from Nancy.

Nancy shrugged. "Oh, I just wanted to help," she said. "I like Ginger. And besides, I didn't have a date for tonight."

"Lots of kids don't have dates," Gloria pointed out. She got out her comb, and then stared at her reflection in the mirror. Something was wrong.

"Yes, but that doesn't help," Nancy said, with a heavy sigh, "especially after hearing about Sam's phone call." She came over to stand behind Gloria and fix her hair. "Hey, the Carrol twins' act was great," she added. "You and your pendant made quite a hit."

Suddenly Gloria realized what was wrong, and she stared at her reflection in openmouthed horror. The sapphire pendant was gone!

Chapter Fourteen

"It's gone!" Gloria gasped, fear spreading through her like an icy wave. "Oh, my God, it's gone!"

"What's gone?" Nancy asked. "What's the matter with you, Gloria?" She looked at her closely. "Oh, no. You've lost your pendant!"

Gloria's knees felt wobbly. "Where could I . . . How could it have . . ." Her throat felt tight, and she was having trouble breathing.

Nancy put her hand on Gloria's arm. "Hey, are you okay?" Nancy pushed Gloria down onto a stool in front of the mirror. "You look kind of pale."

Gloria stared up at her, wide-eyed. "Oh, Nancy! What am I going to do?" she cried. She covered her face with her hands and began to sob wildly. "Maybe I didn't fasten it right when I put it back on after the magic show." She swallowed hard. "Oh, Nancy, it's horrible! How can I face Mrs. Belvedere? She doesn't even know I—" She stopped.

Nancy's eyes widened. "Gloria, you didn't borrow it without *permission*, did you?"

Gloria nodded. "I know I shouldn't have," she confessed in a trembling whisper, "but it was the perfect piece of jewelry for the dress. And it was just for one night, so I figured that it wouldn't matter. I planned to put it back first thing in the morning. Mrs. Belvedere wouldn't even know I had borrowed it. Oh, Nancy, what am I going to *do*?"

"Well, we've got to look for it, of course," she said practically. "In fact, it would probably be a good idea if we asked *everybody* to look for it." She gave Gloria a hopeful smile. "Chances are that we'll find it on the floor, lying just where it fell off."

Gloria sighed and got up, feeling very shaky. "Well, I guess we'd better get started."

Tim was waiting for her outside the rest room. When he saw her, his eyes widened with concern. "What's wrong?" he asked immediately.

"It's the pendant," Gloria said. "It's gone."

"Oh, wow," Tim breathed. He laughed a little. "I've been so busy staring at you, I didn't even notice. Where should we start looking?"

"I have no idea. Nancy's asking Ms. Richards to announce that it's lost, so everybody can help us look."

When the next dance was over, Ms. Richards climbed up on the stage to make her announcement. "Could I have your attention, everybody," she began. "Gloria Larsen has lost a valuable pendant. I'm sure you all noticed it when Mark and Matthew were using it in their magic act. Will everybody please take a few minutes to look around for it?"

People began to scour the room, searching for the pendant. Gloria felt terrible. The magic had disappeared from the evening, and an ugly reality had loomed up in its place. She and Tim searched the dance floor, the game room, and the dining room. The pendant was nowhere to be found. After a while, people stopped searching and went back to dancing.

"Come on, Gloria," Tim said, "let's get something to drink and go out on the deck for a while? Maybe we'll think of someplace else to look."

Heavy with misery, Gloria followed Tim to the bar where a boy in a white jacket was dispensing soft drinks. Shannon was there with Glenn at her elbow. She gave Gloria a shy smile. "I think I know what might have happened to your necklace," she said casually, putting a straw into her soda.

"What?" Gloria exclaimed.

"Well, I can't prove anything, of course," Shannon said, "but I ran into your friend Angie in the rest room a few minutes ago. She was putting something into her purse that she didn't want me to see. She had been looking at it, but when she caught me watching her, she pushed it down inside, as if she didn't want me to see it, and then she ran out of the room." Shannon laughed a little and licked her straw. "If I were a suspicious person, I'd say that Angie probably picked up your necklace from wherever you dropped it. I bet it's in her purse this very moment."

Gloria bristled. "I don't believe a word of it," she said hotly. "Angie wouldn't do a thing like that! If she found the pendant, she'd give it back to me. She's a very honest person."

"Well, she might be a very 'honest person,' " Shannon said, mimicking Gloria's tone, "but her brother is certainly a shady character. What was he doing up here today, anyway? Trying to borrow money from Angie?"

Gloria stared at her. "No, of course not. That's silly. He . . . he . . ." What *had* Tony wanted? Why had he driven all the way up to Rainbow Lake? Angie had never really told them.

"If her brother needed money, Angie would probably do anything to help him, wouldn't she?" Shannon asked smoothly. "She seems to be a very loyal person."

"Well, yes, of course she's loyal. That's one of the nicest things about her. But she would never . . ."

"Loyalty makes people do weird things sometimes," Shannon observed. "It might even make a person steal."

"Shut up, Shannon," Glenn said suddenly.

Shannon turned to face him, her mouth dropping open. "What did you say?" she demanded.

"I said shut up!" Glenn repeated emphatically. "You don't have any proof for what you're saying, and your talk is bound to hurt Angie. Don't you know that a person is innocent until proven guilty?" He crossed his arms and frowned at her. "And anyway, I agree with Gloria. Angie isn't the kind of person who would steal—for *any* reason."

"I don't know what evidence *you've* got for that statement, Glenn," Shannon said, turning away. "Just because she's pretty and she acts so innocent and helpless when you're around . . ."

"You know, Shannon," Glenn said coolly, "sometimes I get fed up with your snobbishness. And right now is one of those times." He turned on his heel and walked away.

Shannon stood there, white faced and shaking with anger. Then she turned to Gloria and said, in a low, bitter voice, "I *know* she was hiding something. I wouldn't be surprised if you found your precious necklace in your friend's purse." The smile on her face was tight and mean. "Why don't you ask her to show you what she's got in there? If she's innocent, of course she'll be glad to let you look."

"I don't have to ask Angie anything," Gloria said, turning away. "I *know* she doesn't have the necklace." Fighting tears, she went out on the deck and leaned over the rail. The full moon threw a bright, silvery light over the lake, deepening the shadows of the trees.

"Here, drink this," Tim said, coming up behind her with a soda. "You'll feel better."

Gloria took a sip of the cold, sweet liquid and pushed it away. "Thanks," she said dully. "I don't think I want anything right now."

"Listen, Gloria, I know it's a valuable piece of jewelry, but your parents probably have it insured. And if they don't . . . well, I'm sure they'll forgive you. After all, you didn't *mean* to lose it. It's not as if you did anything wrong." He slipped his arm around her shoulders.

Gloria pulled away. "There's something you don't know, Tim," she said dully. The shadow of the huge pine tree beside the deck fell between them, as dark as the guilty secret she had been keeping. But she couldn't keep it to herself any longer. The time had come to tell him.

"What don't I know?"

Gloria took a deep breath. "The necklace—it isn't mine," she said, in a dry, flat voice. "I borrowed it from Mrs. Belvedere without telling her. And Mrs. Belvedere isn't my aunt, either. We're not related at all. I just work there. I'm just the twins' baby-sitter." Her voice cracked, as a sob threatened to push through. "I'm not who you think I am, Tim. My family is pretty ordinary. We don't have a lot of money or any social position." The tears welled up in her eyes. "In fact, there's nothing remarkable about us. We're just ordinary people."

For a minute, Tim was silent. *What have I done?* Gloria thought miserably. *If he doesn't hate me for what I've said, he'll surely hate me for not saying it sooner.* She began to cry silently, the tears trickling slowly down her cheeks.

Tim reached into his pocket and pulled out his handkerchief. "Here, let me," he said gently, tipping her face up and wiping the tears from her cheeks. "It's okay, Gloria. Really it is."

Gloria was dumbstruck. "It's okay?" she finally stammered.

"Of course it's okay," Tim said. "Come on, Gloria, what kind of a person do you think I am?" He took both her arms and pulled her toward him. "It's *you* I care about, Gloria, not your parents or your social position or your money. None of that matters to me. I've seen too many people who are interested in other people only for what they can get out of them. And I've learned, the hard way, that you can't tell *anything* about a person by looking at what they own or how they dress or what kind of car they drive." He chuckled. "Anyway, after the way I deceived you in the beginning, wouldn't you say we're even? We may have done the wrong thing in not telling each other the truth when we met, but we fell in love for all the right reasons."

"But I thought . . . I mean, last night you were talking about all the things your parents . . ."

"Sure, I go along with them, if it works out that way. But I'm my own person. I make my own choices." His voice dropped to a husky whisper. "And I choose you."

Gloria began to cry again, but her tears were not tears of desperation, they were tears of hope and relief. If Tim could accept her . . . But suddenly she remembered the pendant.

"What am I going to do about the necklace?" she asked tearfully. "Do you think Mrs. Belvedere will press charges?"

Tim shook his head. "I doubt it," he said. "If we don't find the necklace, I'll go with you to explain things to her." He hugged her. "Now, do you think you could wipe your eyes and blow your nose? I'd like to dance with you again before this night is over."

Gloria looked up at him, her eyes shining as he led her back to the dance floor.

Angie stood watching the dancing couples turn and sway in the dim light. So far, the evening wasn't turning out quite the way she had hoped it would. Suddenly she felt a strong hand on her shoulder. "Will you dance with me?" Glenn asked, in a low voice.

Angie gulped and nodded. They went out onto the dance floor, and she lost herself in Glenn's strong embrace, in the feel of his arms wrapped around her, in the light touch of his breath against her cheek. Her pulse was pounding in her throat, and she was sure her insides were melting.

"Dancing is just an excuse for holding you," Glenn said finally, reaching down to smooth her hair with the palm of his hand. "I've been wanting to do this all weekend."

Angie felt herself blushing. "Me, too," she whispered.

As they danced together in silence, Angie leaned against him, wanting this magical closeness to go on forever. "Want to take a walk on the beach?" Glenn said at last. "There's a full moon tonight."

"I'd love to," she answered. "Just let me get my purse."

Glenn went out on the deck to wait for Angie. Just as she stooped to pick up her purse, Shannon and three other girls came up behind her.

"We demand to see what's in your purse," Shannon said, in a belligerent voice.

"What?" Angie asked, dismayed.

"We know you're hiding something," Shannon said. "And it just might be Gloria Larsen's necklace." She reached for the purse. "Let's see what you're so anxious to hide."

Angie tightened her hold on the purse. "No!" she said. "There's nothing in my purse. I don't have anything to hide."

"Come on, Angie, be reasonable," one of the other girls prodded. Angie recognized Margie, one of Shannon's bunkmates. "If you don't have anything to hide, you shouldn't be afraid to let us look." She put her hand on Angie's arm.

"You're *not* looking in my purse!" Angie said angrily.

Margie shrugged and turned to Shannon. "Well that sounds like an admission of guilt to me."

"To me, too," Shannon said triumphantly. "Now we *know* she's got something to hide." She grabbed Angie's arm and shook the purse loose. Angie watched in horror as Margie turned it upside down, spilling the contents out on the floor.

Loose change bounced in all directions, followed by an eye-shadow palette, wadded-up tissues, a comb with several missing teeth, a tiny flashlight, Gloria's pink lip gloss, and the picture of Glenn that Lani had taken that afternoon. Angie felt so exposed to have her privacy being invaded. Now everyone would know how she felt about Glenn. She felt as though she'd been stripped naked in front of the whole roomful of people.

"Hey, what's going on here?" Gloria stepped up behind Angie.

"We're just looking for your necklace, but I don't see it," Margie explained.

Shannon got down on her hands and knees. "I'm *sure* it's here somewhere," she said. She picked up the photo of Glenn and stared at it in silence for a moment. Then she looked up at Angie, as the realization of it dawned on her. "It was the *picture* you were hiding from me, wasn't it?" she demanded. "You've got a crush on Glenn, and you didn't want me to see that you had a picture of him. That's it, isn't it?" She stood up, waving the photo.

Fighting tears, Angie snatched the photo from Shannon's hand. Without a word, she knelt and scooped the pile of loose things into her purse—

except for the lip gloss, which she handed silently to Gloria. She knew she was about to cry. But she couldn't let them see it. She couldn't let them know that they had gotten to her. Without a word, she turned and bolted through the door, down the front steps, and out into the silvery moonlight.

With the moonlight spilling its trembling, ghostly light over her shoulder, Angie fled as fast as she could down the shadowy path toward the lake. Behind her, she could hear heavier footsteps pounding, and she knew that it must be Glenn, coming after her. But the knowledge only made her run faster. Anything between the two of them was utterly hopeless. She had known that from the very beginning. She had been a fool to let herself start to hope for anything else. Glenn was attracted to her. She had to admit that, especially when she remembered the tender way he had held her on the dance floor. And they might even be friends for a while. But pretty soon, if he stuck with her, his friends would begin to ignore him. And then he would realize that a lot of friends were more important than just one.

Her breath rasped in her throat, her heart pounded like a trapped bird in her ribcage, and her legs felt as if they had enormous lead weights fastened to them. But she kept on going, as fast as she could—

until she tripped over a tree root and went sprawling in the middle of the path.

She lay there, unable to get up in her misery. Glenn caught up with her then and bent down to cradle her tenderly in his arms. "Angie, Angie," he whispered, his lips against her hair, "why were you running away?"

Angie began to cry. "Because they all think I'm a thief," she sobbed.

"You shouldn't care what Shannon and her friends think. After what they did, *they're* the ones who looked bad. And you know that *I* don't think you're a thief."

Angie nodded.

"Why were you running away from me?" Glenn asked.

"Don't you see?" she gasped wildly, struggling to sit up. "I can only embarrass you, make you feel ashamed. You know what kind of family I come from. You know my reputation. Everybody at Glenwood looks up to you and respects you. How would it look to them if you and I were friends?"

"From where I stand," Glenn said softly, "it would look pretty good. Anyway," he went on, "I never would have thought that you would be so prejudiced."

Angie stared at him, shocked. "Me? Prejudiced?

What are you talking about?"

Glenn laughed. "Well, you must be prejudiced against kids like me if you think we're all looking down on you. *I* never believed any of those stupid stories about you. And I know a lot of other people didn't either." He helped her up. "It's just another kind of prejudice," he said softly, "for you to assume we're all alike."

"I don't get it," Angie said.

Glenn put his arm around her, and they began to walk back toward the lodge. "I don't either," he confessed. "I don't have any idea what's going to happen in the future. I just know that if my mind is closed, some opportunities are going to be closed to me, too." He stopped and turned her toward him. "I wish you would open your mind and let your guard down a little, Angie," he said gently, "long enough to see that there are lots of people who really like you."

Angie stared up at him in the moonlight, her eyes still full of tears. "Oh, Glenn, I'll try," she said. And then he kissed her, sweetly and tenderly, and she knew that he meant what he said.

Chapter Fifteen

Instead of going back to the lodge, Angie and Glenn went to the deserted wooden dock, where they took off their shoes and dangled their bare feet in the warm water. The moon and the waves created silent, shifting patterns, and for a long time they sat there, their hands touching. Angie felt as serene as the scene before her.

Finally Glenn yawned and stretched, then stood up. "It must be nearly midnight," he said. "I'm really beat. I think I'd better head for the sack." He knelt behind her and folded both arms tenderly around her waist, burying his face against her hair. "Can I walk you to your cabin?"

Angie shook her head. "I'm not very sleepy," she said. "I think I'll just stay here awhile longer."

Glenn kissed her and stood up. "I'll see you at breakfast, then," he said. "Good night, Angie."

"Good night, Glenn," she said and watched him walk away into the darkness, whistling, his hands in his pockets. She could hardly believe it. Glenn St. Clair really cared about her! And from now on, she didn't intend to deny it. She would have to learn to believe in herself—believe that people could like her, maybe even love her, despite what her family had done.

Angie pulled her feet up under her and sat cross-legged on the dock for a long time, staring out at the silvery ripples. She didn't have a watch, but she knew that it was late—maybe even past the time for Stephanie's usual cabin check—and that she ought to go back to her bunk and try to sleep. Her friends would be wondering what had happened to her. But she couldn't stop thinking about Gloria's lost pendant. She had seen the devastation and despair on Gloria's face when Ms. Richards had announced that it was lost.

Angie felt a prickle of apprehension. If the pendant never turned up, there would still be a lot of people—including Shannon and her friends—who would continue to believe that *she* had taken it and hidden it somewhere. They would never be convinced just because it hadn't been in her purse when Shannon dumped it, and they would keep on spreading the word that she was a thief. Unless the necklace was found, *her* name wouldn't be cleared. And even though she knew that Glenn cared for her no matter what, it would be awful if he had to defend her against those kinds of rumors all the time.

Frowning, Angie sat in deep thought for a few minutes. With so many people looking for the pendant, why hadn't it turned up? What could have happened to it? Then, with sudden determination, she put on her shoes. It was very late, and everyone in the camp was asleep. She scrambled to her feet and started up the rocky path toward the empty lodge. She had to find Gloria's pendant.

The lodge porch creaked noisily when Angie stepped on it, and she jumped. If there *was* anybody around, she didn't want them to hear her or see her. She bent over and slipped off her shoes, glancing around. There was nobody in sight.

Inside, the lodge was as dim and shadowy as the interior of a cave, and just as spooky. Coals still burned in the big stone fireplace in the main room, glowing like malevolent red eyes in the darkness, and nearby a loose shutter banged in the chilly night breeze. Angie began to search every inch of the floor, shining her flashlight along all the baseboards, looking under every piece of furniture—even turning the loose cushions out of the sofa and the chairs. She paid careful attention to the area where Gloria had been sitting after the magic act. Was it possible that she hadn't fastened the catch securely when she put the pendant back on? Angie found nothing.

When she had finished thoroughly searching the main room, she went into the game room. On her hands and knees, she shone her flashlight over the floor. After another long search, Angie had to admit that the necklace wasn't in either of those two rooms. Wearily, she went into the dining room and searched there, concentrating on the area around the piano, where Gloria had been sitting. Nothing.

There was only one place left to look. She glanced out the huge glass window at the deck where the shadows of the pine trees created eerie pools of inky darkness. The deck was built out of wooden planks with spaces between. If Gloria had lost the necklace there, it would probably never be found. And that's where it must be. It certainly wasn't anywhere in the lodge.

Angie turned off her flashlight and sank down on the piano bench, exhausted. She didn't know what time it was, but she thought it must be nearly one o'clock. The moonlight streamed in through the windows, shrouding the room with silver, and in the dim light, the ivory keys of the piano gleamed. With one finger, Angie began to pick out the melody of "Puff the Magic Dragon," humming to herself and remembering how good it had felt when she'd sung with Rayne and Paul. She wondered again if they would work out their differences. She hoped that they would, and that the three of them would be able to sing together again when school started.

Plunk! Suddenly, one of the piano keys made a strange metallic noise, as if it was hitting something other than the string. Angie pressed the key again. Suddenly she stood up, remembering with growing excitement that Gloria had been sitting on the piano earlier in the evening. Was it possible that the necklace had fallen off and tumbled down somewhere *inside* the piano? With trembling hands, she raised the piano lid and shone the narrow beam of the flashlight onto the hammer of the key that had made the strange sound. And there it was, sparkling in the light, lodged against the string: Gloria's necklace!

Jubilantly, Angie tucked the pendant into her purse. Gloria would be so happy! She couldn't wait to get back to the cabin and wake her up and tell her the good news. She started across the dining room toward the deck, carrying her shoes in her hand. Suddenly, she stopped. There, against the window, was an ominous cluster of moving shadows, pressed to the glass. Her heart jumped into her throat, and she clutched her purse tightly.

"Who's there?" she called out in a trembling voice. The shadows blurred and separated. She heard the sliding glass door opening and the sound of footsteps.

Suddenly a blinding torch shone in Angie's face. She put up her hand to shield her eyes against the sharp light. "Well, hello there, Angie," Shannon Welles said, stepping out of the darkness with the torch in her hand.

Angie swallowed. Behind Shannon she could see the shadowy figures of two other girls wearing sweat suits, wet towels draped over their shoulders. She tried to speak, but her mouth was too dry, and nothing came out.

Shannon handed the torch to one of the other girls and stepped forward. "What an interesting evening this is turning out to be," she said coolly. Her bantering tone had a razor-sharp edge. "Now, what do you suppose our little friend Angie is doing sneaking around the lodge with her shoes off? What do you suppose she's been up to?"

"Cabin check!" Stephanie called, poking her head into the door of the cabin. "Is everybody accounted for? Does anybody need anything?" It was after midnight, the lights were out, and the girls were in their bunks.

"Yes," Gloria said, in a sleepy voice. "We're all accounted for. No, we don't need anything. Good night."

"Good night," Stephanie said. "Sweet dreams. See you at breakfast." She closed the door.

When the sound of Stephanie's footsteps faded, Gloria sat bolt upright and tossed off the blankets. "Well, I don't know about the rest of you," she announced to the dark, "but I'm worried." In the shadows, she could just make out the rolled-up pillow under the rumpled blanket on Angie's bed. It was an old trick, but it had been realistic enough to fool Stephanie into thinking that it was *Angie* in the bunk, sound asleep.

"I'm worried, too," Nancy said, from her lower bunk. "Angie isn't the type to stay out after cabin-check time. She always follows the rules. Something must be wrong."

"Right," Lani agreed. "She's been the first one ready for bed every night."

"Who saw her last?" Rayne asked with concern.

"I guess I did," Gloria acknowledged. "She was running out of the lodge after Shannon dumped her purse on the floor to see if she had the pendant."

She got up, groping in the dark for her sweat pants. If Angie was in trouble, it was *her* fault. If she hadn't lost the pendant, Shannon wouldn't have attacked Angie. And then Angie wouldn't have run out of the lodge the way she did. She tied the string of her pants and reached for her sweat shirt. "She looked so upset," she added, "especially when she saw that I noticed my lip gloss on the floor. I knew she assumed I thought she'd stolen it. But I knew that she'd just borrowed it." *The way I borrowed the pendant,* she thought to herself. She pulled her sweat shirt over her head. "I was going to go after her, but Glenn had already started out. I figured he wanted to be alone with her. But that was *hours* ago."

"She must still be with Glenn, then," Lani said.

"Well, if she's with Glenn, there's nothing to worry about," Rayne observed, snuggling down under the blankets. "They're probably sitting down on the dock enjoying the moonlight. We shouldn't interfere." Then she sat up and stared at Gloria. "Where in the world are you going at this time of night, Gloria?" She looked down at her watch, glowing green in the dark. "It's nearly one o'clock."

"I'm going to Glenn's cabin," Gloria said determinedly, "to see if he knows where Angie is."

"You might need help," Lani announced, bouncing out of bed. "I'm going, too. Just give me time to get into my jeans."

"We might as well all go," Nancy said, in a resigned

voice. "We won't get a wink of sleep until you get back, anyway. Come on, Rayne, get up."

The grass was beginning to grow damp and chilly, and the girls' feet were soaked by the time they got to Cypress Creek. The moonlight was bright enough for them to spot the rocks they needed to step on to cross the creek, but Gloria managed to slip and land right in the icy water. As quietly as they could, they made their way to Glenn's cabin and stood under the open window.

"*Ppss-ss-t,* Glenn," Gloria hissed. "Are you there?"

There was no answer. Then a thick, sleepy voice responded. "Who's there? What time is it? What do you want?" There was a pause, and then the voice grew fuzzy and indistinct. "Go away."

"Glenn, it's Gloria Larsen," Gloria said urgently. "We're looking for Angie. Do you know where she is?"

A tousled head appeared at the window. "Angie?" Glenn asked, rubbing the sleep out of his eyes. "You mean she's not at the cabin?" He looked around at the anxious girls standing under the window.

Gloria shook her head. In spite of her heavy sweat shirt, she was shivering from the breeze that blew off the lake. "She never came back after the dance. I saw you run out after her. I thought you might know where she is."

"*I* don't know where she is," Glenn said worriedly. "I mean, I know where I left her, but . . ." He broke off. "What time is it?"

Rayne consulted her watch. "It's one-fifteen."

"I left her over an hour ago," Glenn said, "down by the dock. She said she just wanted to sit there for a while before she went to bed." He disappeared from the window. "Wait there," he commanded, in a muffled voice. "I'll be right out."

When Glenn joined them, they forded the creek again and took the path through the woods to the beach. Gloria had never been in the forest at night before, and the gnarled, twisted shadows of the trees filled her with apprehension. In the darkness of the woods, they had to feel their way down the path, bumping into one another and stumbling over rocks. Out on the beach, however, the moonlight made it easier to see where they were going, and they could walk faster. But when they got to the dock, it was empty. There was no sign of Angie. All they could see was a large puddle of water and the not-quite-faded footprints of bare feet.

"Where could she be?" Nancy asked worriedly. "Do you think these are *her* tracks?"

"If they are, she's grown an extra pair of legs or

two," Lani pointed out. She knelt down and inspected the footprints. "Judging from the tracks, it looks as if there were two or three people here."

"Well, maybe somebody else came along to go swimming," Rayne suggested, "and Angie decided to go in, too." She bent over the tracks with Lani. "Then maybe they all went off together."

"No," Glenn said, shaking his head. "Angie didn't have her bathing suit. And she isn't the kind to go skinny-dipping—by herself or with somebody else."

"Well, what now, Sherlock Holmes?" Gloria asked. "Got any bright ideas?"

Glenn looked at the tracks. "It looks to me like the footprints are heading in the direction of the lodge," he said.

"Well, then, let's go," Gloria said.

"I wasn't sneaking around," Angie said, in a very low voice. She looked away, conscious of the fact that she was holding her shoes in her hand. Her heart was pounding, and her knees felt shaky. "I was just..."

"Well, go on," Shannon said pleasantly, taking a step toward her. "What *have* you been up to? We saw you snooping around in the piano, Angie. Were you retrieving something you had hidden there?"

Angie shook her head vehemently and backed up

a step. "No. I was just looking for . . ."

Shannon took another step. "Did you find what you were looking for?"

Angie pulled in a deep, steadying breath. "As a matter of fact, I did," she said, squaring her shoulders and taking a tighter hold on her purse and shoes. She was going to tell the truth, whether they believed her or not. "I found Gloria's necklace in the piano, caught on one of the hammers. It must have fallen off when she was sitting on top of the piano."

Shannon turned to her friends with a crooked smile. "Isn't that amazing?" she asked sarcastically. "Angie Maroni has managed to locate the necklace that everybody spent *hours* searching for. What incredible luck." Her sharp tone stung. "Of course, she found it. It was exactly where she had hidden it. In the piano."

"I didn't *hide* it in the piano," Angie said desperately. "I just *found* it there."

Shannon turned back to face Angie. Her mouth was twisted. "You know," she said, "you might be able to fool Glenn with your innocent act, but you can't fool me. I know you hid the necklace there!" She grabbed Angie's arm with both hands.

"Shannon! Let her go!"

As if she'd been shot, Shannon dropped her hands. "Glenn! What are *you* doing here?"

Glenn stepped forward into the light of the flashlight, Gloria beside him, and Rayne, Nancy, and Lani right behind. "We came looking for Angie," he said. "What are *you* doing here?"

"Margie and Karen and I went for a midnight swim at the dock," Shannon said with a coy smile, edging closer to him. "Then we came to get something to drink out of the soda machine." She looked pointedly at Angie. "Imagine how surprised we were when we caught Angie taking Gloria's necklace out of the piano. She must have stashed it there earlier."

"The necklace!" Gloria stepped forward. "You've got the necklace?"

Angie nodded, searching Gloria's face. Did Gloria think she had hidden it there? "It was in the piano," she said, opening her purse. "Stuck on one of the hammers." She held it out to Gloria. "I didn't take it, Gloria. Honest I didn't. And I didn't take the lip gloss, either. I just borrowed it."

Gloria clutched the pendant tightly. "Oh, I'm so glad to have it back!" she exclaimed.

"Well, what are you going to do now, Gloria?" Shannon asked. "I mean, it's crystal clear. You wouldn't have your necklace back if we hadn't caught Angie taking it out of the piano. She knew it was there all along—she put it there!"

"That's not true," Angie said, turning in desperation to Gloria and Glenn. "After Glenn left me on the dock, I came up here to look for the necklace. I'd been searching for over an hour when I sat down at the piano and started to pick out a melody. One of the notes sounded funny, and then I remembered that Gloria had been sitting on the piano. I opened it up, and that's where I found the pendant." A sob caught in her throat, and she looked pleadingly at Gloria. "You've *got* to believe me," she said. "Every word is true! I didn't steal it!"

Gloria stepped forward and put her arms around Angie. "Oh, Angie, I know it's true! Do you think I would doubt you?" She hugged her hard. "I know you didn't steal it, and I never thought you stole the lip gloss either. Thank you so much for finding it. You saved *my* reputation!"

"You're not looking at all the evidence, Gloria," Shannon persisted.

"Look, Shannon," Gloria said angrily, "you might as well give up. None of us believe that Angie took the necklace. And if you don't shut up, somebody might think that *you* took the necklace and hid it, just so you could put the blame on Angie."

For a second, Shannon stood sputtering, her face flushing bright red. Then, without a word, she turned and left, followed by her two friends.

Glenn put his arms around Angie and hugged her

tightly. "Well, I don't think she'll be bothering you anymore," he said admiringly.

Angie looked around at her new friends. "I'm really glad all of you came looking for me."

"I'm glad *you* came looking for the necklace," Gloria responded. "If you hadn't, it might never have been found."

Lani gave an immense yawn and glanced at her watch. "Hey, you guys," she said, "it's nearly two o'clock. Any minute now, we're bound to turn into mice. I'd sort of like to be in my bunk when that happens."

Chapter Sixteen

"What's that racket?" Nancy asked sleepily.

"It's that stupid woodpecker again," Lani groaned from under her pillow. "I think it's taken up permanent residence on the roof."

Rayne opened her eyes. "Did I just *dream* that Angie found Gloria's necklace and that we found Angie just in time to keep Shannon from attacking her, or did it really happen?"

"It really happened," Gloria said happily. She reached under her pillow. The pendant was still there, safe. And in a little while, it would be even safer, back in Mrs. Belvedere's jewelry box. She swung her feet over the edge of the bunk and looked at everyone. Today was the last day of Senior Orientation Weekend. Had they only been there since

Thursday? So much had happened that it seemed like a century. "Listen, everybody," she said, with sudden determination. "I have a confession to make. I've already told Nancy," Gloria went on. "But now I want to tell the rest of you and get it off my chest." Now that she had learned how important it was to tell the truth, she wanted to be able to tell the *whole* truth, no matter how much it hurt or how stupid it made her look. She didn't want any more deceptions to stand between her and her friends.

"The pendant I was wearing last night," she continued, "wasn't mine." She looked around. How were they going to respond?

Rayne stared at her. "Whose was it, then?"

"It belongs to Mrs. Belvedere," Gloria said, a bright red flush creeping up her neck. "I borrowed it—without telling her."

"Uh-oh," Angie said softly. "Wow."

Gloria looked at Angie. "You know, Angie, it's a funny thing. You were the one who was worried about your reputation, and you hadn't done a thing. *I* was the one who should have been worried. What I did . . . well, there isn't much difference between that and stealing."

"You *did* intend to put the pendant back, though," Nancy pointed out practically. She began to get dressed. "It seems to me there's a pretty big difference between borrowing something and stealing it."

"Well, that's true," Gloria admitted, "but if Angie hadn't found it, how could I have proved that I intended to put it back?"

"You've got a point," Rayne said. She stretched and yawned. "Well, if nobody minds, I'm going to head for the shower. I promised Paul I'd eat breakfast with him this morning."

Angie got up and put on her robe. "Are things better between you and Paul?" she asked Rayne.

Rayne smiled and nodded as she collected her towel and toilet case. "For the time being, at least. Singing together last night reminded us of how great we are together. So we're going to keep on trying."

"I'll walk to the showers with you, Rayne," Nancy offered.

"Is your confession over?" Lani asked Gloria.

"I guess so," Gloria said with a little laugh. She got out of bed and pulled on her jeans. "Everybody seems to be finished listening, anyway."

"Well, that's what happens with confessions," Lani said, putting on her sneakers. "Once the good part is over, there's not much worth listening to." She stood up. "Anyway, it's almost time for breakfast. Are you coming?"

"In a few minutes," Gloria said. "I want to take Mrs. Belvedere's pendant back first." She couldn't wait to be sure that it was safely back where it belonged.

"Well, did everybody have a good time?" Stephanie asked, as they sat down to eat breakfast. The girls from the cabin were joined by Ginger and Elaine. Stephanie grinned and glanced around the table. "Or, as Ms. Richards would say, was it a productive learning experience?"

Ginger leaned forward. "Speaking of Ms. Richards," she said, pointing with her spoon across the dining room, "look at *that.* Does she look like the same Dragon Lady we all knew and loved in biology II?"

Gloria looked. Ms. Richards and Mr. Dawson were sitting close together over a cup of coffee, their hands touching, clearly oblivious of everything that was going on around them. Gloria had to admit Ms. Richards *did* look different. Her hair spilled down over her shoulders, and her face was much softer. She looked happy and at ease.

Ginger shook her head. "Isn't it amazing how love can transform people?"

Stephanie looked around the table again. "Well, what about my question?" she asked. "Have you learned anything important?"

Gloria giggled. "You should have been around last night, Stephanie." She glanced at Angie. "Talk about learning experiences!"

"What happened last night?" Stephanie asked, with interest. "The last time I saw you, everybody was safely in bed."

"Everybody but Angie," Lani remarked, adding milk to her cereal. "What you saw was a rolled-up pillow. The real Angie was out having adventures."

Stephanie looked at Angie. "Adventures? After cabin check?"

Angie flushed.

"What happened," Gloria explained to Stephanie, "was that Angie decided to come up to the lodge with a flashlight and look for the pendant I lost. And she found it," she added triumphantly.

"You found it?" Elaine exclaimed, staring at Angie. "That's marvelous! Where was it? I thought we looked everywhere."

"It was in the piano," Angie said.

"And then, after Angie found the necklace," Gloria went on, "Shannon and some of her friends found Angie."

"But Shannon was in bed when *I* checked her bunk," Elaine said, looking confused. "The lights were out, and everybody was asleep."

"Well, they must have decided to sneak out after cabin check," Gloria said. She giggled. "Or maybe they tried the rolled-up-pillow trick, too."

Ginger turned curiously to Nancy. "What happened when Shannon and her friends found Angie with the necklace?"

Nancy gave a short laugh. "You can guess," she said. "Shannon accused Angie of hiding the necklace in the piano so she could come back later and get it, after everyone was asleep. Actually," she added soberly, "at that point things were beginning to get a little sticky."

"I was lucky that you guys came along," Angie said, buttering her croissant. "If you hadn't, I'm not sure how I would have proved that I didn't take the necklace."

Stephanie shook her head. "This is beginning to sound like the plot of a mystery novel," she said. "A mysterious search in a dark lodge, the discovery of the missing jewelry, a dramatic confrontation with an accuser, and rescue by loyal friends." She looked around the table. "It must have been an exciting night."

Lani yawned. "Yeah," she said, "I'm much too tired to conduct any interviews this morning. Too much excitement."

Ginger laughed. "Say, Lani, how's that going anyway? Have you found the perfect boyfriend yet?"

Lani shook her head. "Not yet. But I've got a pretty good idea of what I'm looking for. And I've been thinking about broadening my data base by including some older men. Do you think Craig would give me an interview?"

Ginger ran her fingers through her hair. "You can always try," she said.

Gloria groaned. "Lani will try *anything*," she said.

"Well," Nancy said, pushing her chair back, "I'm going back to the cabin to pack."

"I'll come with you," Gloria said, picking up her tray. They took their dishes to the counter. "I'm going back to Glenwood on the bus today. My summer job is finally over. Do you want to sit together?"

"Well," Nancy said evasively, not looking at her, "I've already promised to sit with somebody else."

"Who?" Gloria asked blankly.

Nancy looked down at her shoes. "Well, if you must know," she said, "I promised to sit with Dave."

"Dave Carstairs?" Gloria exclaimed. "I thought you were finished with boys."

Nancy's face was bright red. "Oh, I am," she said quickly. "We're just going to talk about *The Call*, that's all. He has some good ideas for feature articles."

Gloria laughed. "Well, have fun," she said.

"Gloria!"

Gloria looked up and saw Tim coming across the room toward her.

"Oh, Tim, I've got the best news!" she cried, running to meet him. "Angie found the pendant last night in the piano! I've already taken it back to the Belvederes'."

Tim hugged her. "That's great," he said, sounding relieved. He led her into the deserted main room. "I just found out that my folks are going to drive to Glenwood today. You want to come with us?"

Gloria thought about her deception. "Do your parents know the truth now?" she asked hesitantly.

Tim nodded. "I told them this morning that we got our identities confused," he said with a chuckle. "It wasn't a big deal with them."

"Okay, then," Gloria decided. "I'll get my things out of the cabin and then go up to the Belvederes' for the rest of my clothes."

"I'll pick you up over there," Tim said. He looked at her. "You know, Gloria, this has been a tremendous weekend. And the funny thing is that even though we're getting ready to leave, it doesn't feel that it's ending." He looked at her intently. "Do you have that feeling?"

"Yes," she whispered. "I do."

Everyone but Angie had gone to the cabin to pack. She wanted to look at the lake one last time. She walked down to the beach and sat on the dock, looking across the sparkling water toward the cliff where

Glenn had killed the snake and thinking about everything that had happened over the last few days. Gloria and Tim had cleared away all their deceptions. Rayne and Paul were working on their misunderstandings. Nancy and Lani both had big ideas about their projects for the year ahead. And—most amazing of all—she and Glenn were becoming friends. She felt so different from when she arrived. If senior year was anything like the last few days, she would be completely transformed by the end of the school year.

"A penny for your thoughts," Glenn said softly.

Angie jumped. "You startled me!"

"Sorry," Glenn said. He squatted down beside her on the dock. "The girls at the cabin said you were down here." He looked across the lake. "It's pretty during the day," he added. "But I think I like it better in the moonlight." He put his hand on her shoulder and they watched the lake in a companionable silence.

When they stood up to go, Glenn took her hand. "Will you sit with me on the bus?" he asked hesitantly.

Angie took a deep breath, remembering how lonely she had been on the trip to the lake, watching all the other couples. Now *she* was going to be part of a couple—and with the boy she had dreamed about for almost six months. It was unbelievable. "I'd love to," she said happily.

"But there's a catch," Glenn went on, with a sober look.

"A catch?" Angie asked in dismay.

"You have to promise to get in through the door. I know you like climbing in and out of windows, but this time I have to insist."

With a grin, he ducked the punch that Angie aimed at his shoulder, and the two of them ran together up the path.